my dear ␣
and sister in ␣

Delight yourself in the Lord,
And He will give you the
desire of your heart. Psalm 57:4

Thank you, Jesus.

Annie Myrtle Deas
2-15-06

Hostage

by

Annie Myrtle Deas

authorHOUSE™

1663 LIBERTY DRIVE, SUITE 200
BLOOMINGTON, INDIANA 47403
(800) 839-8640
WWW.AUTHORHOUSE.COM

First published by AuthorHouse 12/08/05

ISBN: 1-4208-8954-0 (sc)

Printed in the United States of America
Bloomington, Indiana

This book is printed on acid-free paper.

Cover Art by Katie Hewell Yerdon
Copy editing by Bonnie Deas Novak
Compilation of book by N-Y Publishers

Dedication

This book is dedicated to my grandchildren and great-grandchild, whose names appear as characters throughout the story.

Thanks to Martha Hewell for her many hours spent typing the original portions of this book and saving them on disks.

About the Author

A native of Mississippi, Annie Myrtle Deas now lives in Vorea, New York. She has been married to Cecil Deas for more than 50 years and is the mother of three adults, grandmother of seven and recently became a great-grandmother. Both daughters are pastors' wives in Upstate New York, and son, Cecil Mack Deas, Jr., works for New York Life in Maine. An alumna of Moody Bible Institute, Deas taught Sunday School for 55 years and still teaches as a substitute and speaks at women's retreats. She served as a counselor at a Crisis Pregnancy Center where she first encountered some of the issues addressed in this book.

CHAPTER ONE

It was a bright autumn morning as Annie crawled out of bed and stepped to the window of her second story room. She had lived in this house all her life with her parents. Her window looked out on the large backyard where she had spent many hours playing.

Being an only child she had often been lonely, but her parents had been foster parents from time to time for children who had, for some reason or another, to be away from their own home.

Annie often thought of these children as her brothers and sisters. How dear her own parents had always been. They had such love for people, and now it seemed so hard to see how her father had suffered in his endeavor to help the young women and men in their community to realize the devastation of abortion. In his calm, trusting way Andrew Marrow had led the fight against the issue of taking the life of unborn babies.

As Annie breathed the fresh morning air, the fragrance of bacon frying reached her senses and brought her back to the present.

Today was Annie's nineteenth birthday.

Quickly showering and getting dressed in a gray wool skirt and pale pink sweater, Annie brushed her golden blonde hair and tied a tiny

1

pink ribbon around it, letting her hair fall around her shoulders in its natural curl. Her bright blue eyes stared at the girl in the mirror.

"This is your day, Annie Marrow, how are you going to spend it?" she asked her image. Just then she heard the voice of her mother call from the bottom of the stairs.

"Are you ready for breakfast, Annie? Your father has already gone to work, and I'm waiting to have breakfast with you."

"I'm almost ready, Mother," called Annie, as she put the finishing touches on the bed. Annie had been taught to keep her own room from a small child and prided herself in being neat.

Julia Marrow had been a faithful mother and spent time teaching Annie to be well organized with both work and time.

"Happy birthday, Annie." Julia said and hugged her daughter as she came down to the living room.

"Your father hated that he had to leave so early this morning." Julia said. "He had a meeting with the board of the pregnancy care center. I believe that is the only thing that could keep him from having breakfast with you on your birthday. He said he would make it up to you with a surprise later. Do you have any plans for the day after your classes?"

"Only to run by The Boutique and pick up my dress for tonight and two errands of mercy. I am so excited about the plans you and Dad have for me. I shall always remember having dinner at Riverside."

Julia smiled as she turned to butter another piece of toast at the thought of the surprise in store for Annie that was planned for her birthday. Her closest friends, Christina and Katie, were inviting some of Annie's peers to the Riverside Inn for a surprise.

"Mom, what was the telephone conversation about that upset Dad so much last night?" Annie inquired. "I couldn't help overhearing as I was studying in the dining room. It seemed that Dad was really disturbed when he hung up, and I noticed he went up to your suite with his Bible and did not return to say goodnight."

"I believe you know the pressure that has been put on the pregnancy care center board lately by various individuals and agencies."

Annie raised her blue eyes which were filling with tears to look at her mother.

"Yes, I have heard and read about threats and comments made through the media about the crusades against the abortion issue, and especially Dad's plans for a home for pregnant girls and an adoption placement agency."

"It seems one of the board has been made aware of some plans the opposition has to block the efforts of the center to reach teens with the awareness of the danger of abortion and stop construction of the Good Shepherd Home for Women. Some of these threats are causing fear to grip members of the board's families," Julia remarked.

"Are you afraid?" Annie asked, thoughtfully.

"Not really afraid, Annie, but a little anxious at times. Your father is one of the most known leaders in this movement. We spent much time and prayer before we got involved. We have claimed God's promises often. We have known all along that when you go against Satan, he gets mad and doesn't fight fair." Julia stirred her coffee, not raising her tear-filled eyes to look at Annie.

"Your father is well aware of the danger from Satan's forces against him. He doesn't believe any harm will come to us," she added.

Annie put her dishes in the dishwasher and kissed her mother on the cheek. "I better hurry, Mother, my class starts in fifteen minutes, and I don't want to be late. I'll see you around three. Is there anything you need me to pick up for you?" Annie was slipping into her jacket as she picked up her books and started for the door.

"No, dear, I have to go in this morning so I can take care of those things. Have a great day, Annie. I love you." Julia waved as Annie closed the door behind her.

Annie arrived at Jefferson Community College a few minutes early, and, realizing that in her haste she had failed to take time for her devotional, she sat in the car and read Ephesians, chapter six. Her eyes were riveted to the twelfth verse . . . "We wrestle not against flesh and blood, but against principalities, against powers, against the rulers of the darkness of this world, against spiritual wickedness in high places".

Looking through the windshield without seeing, she saw that the truth of her mother's words were verified by this verse.

"Dad is wrestling against darkness and spiritual wickedness in a very real way," she whispered. "Dear God, protect my dad against these evil forces, and make his life and work glorify You in the most beneficial way. Thank you, Jesus, for the love You have brought into many lives through my parents. Amen."

Annie looked at her watch to find that she had three minutes to get to class. Hurriedly, she left her New Testament on the seat, locked her car and made a dash for her Algebra 103 class. She slipped into her desk just as Professor Moore began her instructions. Annie's mind tended to wander to the events of the approaching evening as well as the conversation she had shared with her mother. Normally Annie was a most attentive student.

Finally, class was over and Annie prepared to leave the classroom when someone shouted to her, "Happy birthday, Annie Marrow."

Turning, Annie caught sight of Nathan Whitten, dark hair curled neatly about his head and his dark eyes bright with laughter.

"Nathan, what are you doing here?" Annie asked.

Christina and Nathan had been dating quite regularly for the past six months, and since Christina and Annie were best friends, she had been in Nathan's presence very often. She liked Nathan. He had been with Christina to Bible study on a number of occasions.

"I'm here to pick Christina up for lunch. Have you seen her?" Nathan inquired.

"Oh, yes, she and Katie were here just a few minutes ago. Perhaps she is still in class. I'll see you soon, I hope." Annie smiled and started to the elevator. Nathan watched her as she turned in the elevator, thinking how surprised Annie was going to be at Riverside when the many friends showed up to celebrate her birthday. Annie was so easy to love. Although she was quiet with people she had just met, she was a lot of fun with her friends. She was such a caring person.

As Annie stepped out of the elevator, she spotted a group of her friends, laughing and talking. She knew if she got involved in their conversation, she would lose a lot of the time that was so valuable to her today. She needed to go somewhere for lunch as soon as she went to The Boutique and in her involvement, in her plans for the day, she tried to slip out with just a brief hello.

"Annie," Kimberly called. "I do hope you have a happy birthday. I'm sorry I can't do something special with you today. You know how my classes run on Friday. Perhaps we can celebrate another day." Kimberly had to smother a smile as she thought of the grand party she was looking forward to attending that very evening for Annie. The others waved as they hurried to class with a chorus of happy birthdays.

Annie thought how blessed she was with caring friends as she walked to her little Toyota. She smiled as she reflected on the many times they all had shared.

Mr. and Mrs. Marrow had always welcomed people into their home, and the young people of Watertown had found a haven there. It was not unusual to have one or two spend-the-nighters during the week and on weekends. Andrew Marrow, a vice-president of a local firm, often spent hours of his leisure time counseling in the various centers available, and his home was a favorite place for those in need of guidance to come and find compassion as well as themselves. Julia had often remarked that she never knew whom she might find on her sofa in the family room when she awoke in the morning.

It was a beautiful fall day. The trees were beginning to change and in just a few days would become a brilliant blaze of color. The campus always was a picture postcard at any time of the year but especially in this season.

Annie turned the lock of her car door unaware of the shiny dark blue Park Avenue pulling up in the space behind her. A car door slammed, and a tall man dressed in a navy sport coat and grey pants approached her car. His tie was a conservative print of maroon, navy and grey. Annie had always been intrigued by men's clothes. She had often helped her mother select clothes for her father.

The strange young man stepped briskly to her side and, as she looked up, he smiled a rather awkward smile.

"You are Miss Annie Marrow, are you not?" he asked with a little nervousness in his voice.

"Yes, I am," Annie replied with a small amount of surprise.

"Your father wants you to meet him for lunch," the young man said, avoiding her eyes.

Annie, remembering the times her father had sent one of his assistants to pick her up to meet him for lunch or for a snack somewhere unexpectedly, looked up and tried to meet his eyes.

"You must be Kip Thornton, Dad's new assistant." The man's eyes brightened at this, and he smiled and nodded his head in agreement.

Annie thought how like her father this was. He failed to be able to have breakfast with her, and now he had been very creative with that promised surprise.

"Let me lock my car, will you, and we shall be on our way."

Annie missed the look of triumph on the face of the tall stranger as he patiently guided her toward his car. He was most courteous to help her into the car and rushed around to the driver's side. Slipping his long legs in behind the steering wheel, he sped away from the curb. He was half-smiling thinking how easy Miss Marrow had made this assumption.

CHAPTER TWO

Julia was singing as she wrapped the gold and sapphire tennis bracelet for the big surprise party for Annie.

"She has been such a blessing to us," she murmured out loud to herself, "Even if she does have a little spitfire temper."

Julia chuckled as she remembered the times they had disagreed on minor things, and Annie had displayed her opinions vehemently. The amazing thing about Annie was her ability to work out her frustrations by turning to God's Word and letting the Word reveal to her when she was in error. Her willingness and readiness to ask forgiveness from both God and those to whom she had demonstrated her anger was one of her strong character traits. A smile played around Julia's lips as she thought of the beautiful friends and their devotion to Annie. The phone rang, and Julia picked it up.

"Hello," Julia said.

"Hello, Mrs. Marrow, this is Christina. I just had to call to tell you that when I saw Annie this morning, she seemed to be so unaware of our plans at Riverside. She was telling me about her father not having breakfast with her and that she was having dinner out tonight. Katie and I did not give it away. All the gang is so happy about surprising

Annie. She is so special to us."

"You are special to her also," Julia said. "I am excited about the party. Did Katie check on the cake? Her aunt makes the most beautiful ones and delicious too. Annie often speaks of the chocolate cake she made for Katie's birthday. You girls have been invaluable in planning this event. Thank you."

"The cake is in the making. We made sure it was chocolate and decorated with a lot of pink roses. I am sure it will be scrumptious. I can almost taste it now. Katie also asked the restaurant to bring it out on a pink tablecloth so that it would show up to its best," Christina laughingly replied.

"Annie will be so pleased. I can see her bright blue eyes shining now. Oh, by the way, did you hear from Tony? He wanted to be there so badly. I've been unable to reach him. He seems to care for Annie even though she is not as taken with him at the moment."

"Yes, he was most enthusiastic about coming, and in fact he has a great present for her . . . a beautiful sapphire pendant on a tiny chain. I was afraid he was pushing things too much, but he would have it no other way. Well, I better run and finish all these chores before time to dress for the party." Christina hung up and Julia finished the bow on the present.

Hmm, it would be wonderful to see Annie interested in such a nice man as Tony Harvey. He was so faithful to church and took a great interest in all the activities. Julia had never interfered in Annie's choice of friends . . . she had never had to before.

Three o'clock is rushing to arrive, thought Julia, as she pressed her dress for the evening. Annie would be driving into the driveway very soon. She was always so punctual, a trait she acquired from her father. He had always made it so important to be on time. His reasoning was that when you are late you are saying to the other person your time is no consequence to me. During Annie's early childhood, being late and failing to keep a promise had been punishable, unless unavoidable.

Julia rushed into the suite and began to lay out Andrew's clothes for the evening. She wanted everything to be just right with no slip-ups. She lost count of time as she pressed a shirt of cream cotton and matched a silk tie.

This one would look very nice with his dark suit, she thought.

Hurrying downstairs, she heard Rover barking.

Rover got his name because as a puppy he was forever sniffing around, never still. Annie had been given the puppy on her tenth birthday making Rover about nine years old and a faithful companion to the family. As a rule, he did not bark unless he was in trouble. Julia rushed to the back door to find that Rover had his head stuck through the fence at a place where the palings were broken, and his collar had caught and bound him to the spot. He was putting up quite a fuss over his predicament. Julia was able to lift the paling slightly and pull the collar down, freeing Rover.

"There you are, old boy. You thought you were caught in a trap, didn't you? Annie should be home any minute now. Here, have a treat; that should make you feel better."

As Julia started toward the kitchen door she glanced at her watch . . . three-thirty. *What was keeping Annie?* Perhaps her dress was not ready, Julia reasoned. *I will wait until four o'clock, and if she has not phoned or arrived, I'll phone The Boutique. It is so unlike Annie not to call.*

The telephone was ringing when Julia entered the house.

That must be her now, thought Julia.

"Hello," Julia answered.

"Julia, is everything going well for the party tonight?" Andrew's voice boomed over the lines.

"Well, yes, Andrew, but I am a little concerned about Annie. She was due to arrive home at three o'clock, and it's almost four, and she has not phoned. You haven't seen her, have you? She was to pick up her dress at The Boutique and run an errand or two. Perhaps the traffic was heavier than usual." Julia did not want to worry Andrew unnecessarily.

"So unlike Annie not to call and especially since she knew that we were to go out at seven. She usually likes to spend some time on her books and have a quiet time before dinner. I will be home around four-thirty. We'll hope and pray she is in by the time I get home."

Andrew hung up the phone with a worried look on his face. *We are probably getting disturbed over nothing . . . Annie is nineteen today; she is old enough to manage her own time without the aid of a mother and father; yet, it is so unlike Annie to fail to think that her tardiness would cause her parents to worry.*

Julia dialed The Boutique shortly after four to be told that Annie had as yet not picked up her dress. What did Mrs. Marrow want them to do about it since they would close at five. This information brought a deep frown to Julia's face as she was trying to determine what could have delayed Annie.

"Mrs. Brandon, I'm concerned that Annie has not been by yet," Julia said. "She told me this morning that she was to pick up her dress a little before three o'clock. She hasn't called or anything?"

"Just a moment," placing her hand over the phone, Mrs. Brandon asked the assistant, Miss Thomas, if she had heard from Annie. "Mrs. Marrow, the last time we spoke to Annie was yesterday afternoon, when she called to inquire as to the time her dress would be ready. I'm very sorry. I do hope nothing has happened to Annie in the way of an accident or anything," Mrs. Brandon offered.

"Of course," Julia thought, as she looked up the number of the local hospital. Perhaps Annie had been taken to the emergency room. Julia's friend Linda, who worked as the receptionist there, would tell her if she had been. But upon speaking to Linda, Julia was told that her name was not on the list of the patients.

At the point of tears, Julia heard a car driving into the driveway. Running to the garage door, she saw her husband getting out of the car, not bothering to remove his briefcase.

"Any word, honey?" he asked with a tremble in his voice.

"Nothing, Andrew. I phoned The Boutique, and she has not been there to pick her dress up. They will close at five. What do you think we should do? I also phoned the hospital emergency room and, thank God, she was not on their patient list. What do you make of it?" Julia spoke with nervousness in her voice.

"I'll go back to The Boutique and follow the route Annie normally would drive to the college, would you like to go with me?" Andrew asked.

"I better stay here in case she calls and needs help. I'll also call Mrs. Brandon and ask her to wait in case you are a little after five o'clock arriving there." Julia was holding the tears back from her eyes as she watched Andrew back out of the driveway.

I'm getting all disturbed, and Annie could be perfectly safe. I must pull myself together and go to the only One who knows where Annie is at the present. We have tried to teach Annie in time of trouble to turn to the One Who knows all things, yet here I have been trying to handle the problem in my own strength. Yet, it is so hard when it is your child. God so loved the world, He gave His only son . . . God, you did, didn't you?

Julia knelt beside her sofa and asked God's protection on Annie.

Although praying had not solved the problem, it helped Julia to know that she had taken the problem to the One with power to protect and the only One Who in all probability knew where Annie was at the present. It seemed her heart was a little lighter with Christ bearing the load with her.

The verse, "Lo, I am with you always, even to the end of the world," was one verse she must keep before her. Was she being overanxious? No, no matter where or what was keeping Annie, God knew that her love for her child had prompted her to "Cast all her cares on Him." He wanted to share the load, and He was definitely with Annie wherever

. . . . . .

A car turned into the drive as Julia came out of her presence with the Lord, and she rushed to the window to see, hoping it would be Annie's little Toyota. It was Andrew who came through the garage door with a worried, almost devastated look on his face.

"Her car was parked at the curb in front of Harding Hall. It was locked with her math book and her New Testament on the front seat. I can't understand where she has gone. I inquired about her whereabouts, but no one had seen her since this morning. None of her friends were there. Have you talked with them? I went to The Boutique for her dress . . . I hope she will need it.

"Oh, Julia, honey, God is in control. I kept reminding myself that He knows where Annie is, and He has the power to keep her from harm. I was reminded of the verses in 1 Peter 5:7, 'Casting all your care upon Him; for He careth for you.' I am thankful we have a heavenly Father to go to for help in time of need."

Andrew drew Julia into his arms, and they both wept, consoling each other in their love for each other, for Annie and most of all with their love for God.

CHAPTER THREE

The big car sped through traffic with great ease. The tall stranger was a superb driver, quite experienced in driving in rushing traffic. Watertown was a busy place at this time of day. Streets were lined with maples already dressed in tinted leaves just before the Master Painter finished His fall masterpiece. The sun filtered through the branches forming patterns on the street.

Annie could smell the aftershave worn by the man at her side. It had the fragrance of a very expensive cologne she had sampled in the department store when she was shopping for her dad's birthday. She glanced under her lashes out of the corner of her eye at the tall man. Strange, that her dad had chosen him to pick her up, she thought. He usually sent one of the various older men on an errand of this nature. Perhaps they were busy, and as this was the newest employee at the firm, he had not settled into a rigid schedule as had the others.

He kept his eyes on the street as they sped through the traffic lights. *Where were they going to meet her father?* She wondered. Usually they met at one of the many restaurants on Arsenal Street close to the office so her father would not lose much time away for lunch. *Since this was her birthday, he must have decided to find some place new.*

"You being new at the office, do you enjoy your job, Mr. Thornton?" Annie quizzed, trying to start a conversation.

Obviously the man was rather shy and found it hard to find words to fit the occasion.

"Thus far I have, Miss Marrow. I have found it quite easy," he replied, keeping his eyes on the approaching exit to Interstate 81 South.

Why were they taking the interstate? Annie wondered. *Where on earth was her surprise to be?* She watched the scenery on her side of the highway as it faded into nothingness. Surely he would soon exit and they would be meeting her father. Annie had grown silent and was trying to relax. *What did she have to be concerned about? This man knew where he was supposed to go.*

This was her surprise, and she did not want to be stressed out when lunch finally was served. Her father would not want to cause her concern. He wanted to make this day the happiest. That was the reason he had sent for her. She leaned back against the soft seat and rested her head on the headrest committing herself to the care of this Kip Thornton.

The man glanced at the lovely girl and thought how very trusting she was of her father. Without doubt she had believed him when he had told her that he was to meet her father for lunch. She was really quite beautiful with her golden blonde curls falling on her shoulder and the big, clear, innocent, blue eyes staring at the passing scenery. Her complexion was clear and creamy, untouched by any blemishes, and the pink sweater she wore brought just enough color to her cheeks.

Was what he was doing going to bring harm to this rare young woman? Should he have involved himself in this plan of Jake Ramsey's? Dr. Ramsey had said no harm would come to her; he just wanted to deter Andrew Marrow from his plan to open the pregnancy care center and adoption home for girls who found themselves in a difficult situation.

"I believe every woman should have the choice, have the option readily available and be encouraged to take it if she wants an abortion," he had reasoned. "Adding more choices of actually having the baby and keeping it or putting it up for adoption only confuses the issue at a time when these young women need to make a quick decision," Ramsey had said.

If this Marrow girl's father were allowed to go on with his plan to build the Good Shepherd Home for Women, then confusion over decision-making would prevent these girls from coming to Ramsey for abortions until it was too late to do anything. Ramsey was actually helping the economy of Upstate New York by getting rid of unwanted pregnancies so these young women could go on with their lives, get an education and be productive contributors to the work force. Marrow's idealistic plans would cause a glut of poverty-level children that would drain the already over-taxed middle and upper class of the region. Besides, the kidnapping was only temporary, and Ramsey had promised no harm would come to this young woman.

Yet, there was Louis Chairvollotti. He did not trust him to do what Ramsey promised. He had a hard time keeping his distance with girls and had a tendency to be abusive with them, even the ones who came to Ramsey's office for abortions. *Oh well, that is Ramsey's problem; my job has been to persuade her to come to the Manor. Ramsey said I would stay at the Manor and the three of us, Louis and Steven Billups and myself, would take turns guarding her. Darlene Gray would be around at times. She could be tough to deal with as she wanted to be the center of all men's attention. Perhaps that is why she has had to use Ramsey's services so often. A shaky voice broke into his thoughts . . . had she been speaking to him and he unhearing?*

"Mr. Thornton, how far are we going, and where are we going? This is so unlike my father to go so far from the office just for lunch." She looked a little frightened.

"We will be at your destination shortly," he replied without looking at her. He could not bring himself to look at her frightened eyes. My, she is pretty, he thought. *About twenty minutes before the exit. Then to*

*weave around the small country roads and to the end of the lane. Ramsey
had planned this well. He must know Andrew Marrow would do anything
to keep his daughter from harm. It would be almost impossible to trace
their path to the Manor. Ramsey had even maneuvered someone else into
securing the Manor rather than have it leased in his name. He had covered
his tracks well. He had promised that no harm would come to the girl. He
just wanted to persuade Marrow to stop this project he had undertaken.
When the man relinquished the pursuit, Ramsey planned to release the girl
unharmed. Unless Louis . . .*

She believes me to be this Thornton guy . . . .

Annie was feeling something she had never experienced before--
extreme fear. *Was this new guy to be trusted? Perhaps her father did not
know him as well as he thought he did. Why did he send him? He seemed
unfriendly anyway. He was certainly not a conversationalist. This road is
strange. My, this is almost a lane. How did her father ever find this place?
Would the restaurant ever appear? Had she taken too much for granted?
This man had not actually told her that he was Kip Thornton, only that
her father wanted to have lunch with her. She had assumed he was the
new employee.*

She glanced at the driver. He was dressed respectably enough. His
hair glistened black in the sunshine as it came through the window.
She had noticed his eyes briefly once or twice to be guarded yet dark
brown. Actually he was rather attractive, but there was something
rather unsettling about his manner. He avoided looking her in the eye.
*Was he being honest with her? He looked in good shape physically, probably
worked out regularly. What did he do in his leisure time?* She pondered.

This lane was endless. A beautiful drive, but where did it lead?
They had come quite a distance before turning off on the ever-winding
lane, and no building was yet in sight. A big curve directly in front of
them wound around huge hardwood trees in colors of yellow, orange
and red sprinkled with a few green shades that had not been colored
by the frosty nights. She sighed a shaky sigh and blinked the tears back

from her eyes. Fear was inevitable. Doubts besieged her. *Had she fallen prey to a pick-up? Was she too trusting?* With all these thoughts flitting through her mind causing fear to mount, she saw the Manor. It was certainly isolated. No sign of life around. Where did the cars park that brought the customers to this far-out place?

Turning to the man at the wheel, she asked "Mr. Thornton, are you sure this is the place?"

"Yes, Miss Marrow, this is definitely the place I was told to bring you," he remarked.

He swung in the drive to the side of the huge two-story house painted white with gleaming white trim. The lawn was cut to perfection and seemed to spread to the stream that ran at the back of the sloping terrain. Flowers bloomed in profusion, chrysanthemums in mauves, yellows and bronze. The picture was stunning among the hardwoods blazing with color.

The car had stopped, and the man was opening the door for her to get out. He took her arm. She felt a slight pressure steering her toward the front door. He opened the door and led her inside; reluctantly she took in the large foyer with the gleaming dark wood, polished to a satin finish. The floor was carpeted with a plush carpet of pale mauve. There was a massive staircase lined with dark spindles leading to a second story that had rooms.

She looked questioningly at the man who had brought her here.

Where was her father? Where was she to have lunch? She was very hungry now as it was well after her normal lunch time. A door opened on the right of the foyer, and a man approached them. He had dark hair that was graying at the temples and a familiar face. Where had she seen him?

"Have any trouble, Jason?" he asked the tall man who had driven her here.

"Jason?" Annie questioned. "I thought your name was Kip. Where is my father? Why have you brought me here? My father is not here,

17

is he? How could you do such a thing!"

"I did not tell you my name was Kip," Jason reminded her. "You assumed me to be your father's new employee, Miss Marrow."

He looked at her for the first time, and she noticed a frown crease his brow.

"But who are you?" she asked the man who had entered from the room at the right.

"I, Miss Marrow, am Jake Ramsey. We do not intend to harm you, only get you out of the picture for a few days or how ever long it takes to stop your father in his new endeavor," he said and smiled, but his eyes were hard.

"How dare you do such a horrible thing! Can't you deal fairly with this situation without taking me as hostage to keep your awful business of killing unborn children open?" Annie demanded, unable to control the anger and mixture of fear in her voice. "How do you intend to keep me here?" Annie asked, not really wanting to know the answer.

"That will be no problem, Miss Marrow, as there is nothing in miles of this place, and the stream at the back is quite dangerous at this time of year," Ramsey replied. "Anyway, you will be kept in your suite of rooms and locked in with guards around the clock. We mean to do you no harm if you cooperate.

"Jason, here, and two other guys that you will meet later will guard your suite, seeing that you are comfortable with all the necessities that you will require," he informed her as he turned to go back into the room which looked like a study.

When he reached the door, he turned to Jason, "See that she is made comfortable in her suite, Jason. Steven will be up to relieve you as soon as possible."

With this he closed the door, leaving them in the foyer.

"Please come with me, Miss Marrow," Jason said, as he caught her elbow and propelled her toward the stairs.

What should she do? Is there any way she could escape? This is such an out-of-the-way place. If she could secure the key and leave in the car . . . but how could she get hold of the key?

"We mean to do you no harm if you cooperate," the man had said. Jason was practically pushing her up the stairs.

Annie turned on the stairs and asked, "Why did you get mixed up in all this? You appear to be a very nice young man. Are you also a doctor who is involved in abortions?"

"We mean you no harm, Miss Marrow, but there are some questions you will not have answered." Jason would not look at her but kept urging her nearer the top of the stairs.

If she tried to escape she could be harmed, even killed, although no harm had been planned for her. That would bring more hurt to her parents. Perhaps, if she did as she was told, she would be released soon. She knew her father was worried. *Would he know what had happened to her? Would Ramsey contact him to tell him he had abducted her? What was Ramsey's plan? Was it to frighten her father into giving up his dream of the center? Or was it only to delay it until he could push some legal issue through to stop the building of the center? If only she knew what to do, or at least try to do. What could she do?* She must remain obedient until she knew what would be best. She must not go off on a plan unorganized. The situation could be worse.

Jason opened the door to a huge room. It was beautifully decorated, and Annie would have loved it under any other circumstances. The walls were painted a pale blue with satiny moldings of the same color. There were large windows looking out over the lawn at the back of the house. The curtains were gleaming white and sheer, allowing the sun to shine through. There were blinds to shut out the light or close out the night.

The room was furnished with chairs covered in chintz fabric of blue with white and mauve. All the pieces were of exquisite taste. There was a bedroom which led off the sitting room to the left. It was also blue with wallpaper on one wall in a tiny pattern. On the queen size bed was a coverlet of snowy white with blue and mauve pillows, piled neatly.

Julia would have loved this room . . . "Mother," Annie gasped. How was she going to take all this?

Jason spoke to her from the door. "There are toiletries in the bath, and the closet contains clothes similar to those you have on, I am told, in your size. I am sure you will find everything you will need here. Should you need anything we have not thought of, please tell your guard . . . perhaps I should call him your 'companion' . . . that sounds better, doesn't it?"

Is he wishing he was not involved? Annie wondered. Jason had been most kind in the way he had handled this situation . . . still, he was the one who had abducted her. *Is that not kidnapping? Is he aware of the seriousness of this thing he had done? Does he do this often?*

"I am sure everything is in order, Mr. . . . what is your name again?" Annie turned to face him.

"Just let it go as Jason, for the time."

She made a step from the bedroom toward the sitting room, and suddenly her legs seemed unable to hold her up. Jason, watching her, rushed to her side to steady her. He looked intently at her silky blonde hair as her head touched his arm.

She was wearing a delicious-smelling cologne. Suddenly he realized she must be hungry. In all the excitement, he had forgotten she had not eaten. She had thought she was being taken to meet her father for lunch.

"I will ring the kitchen for your meal," he said. "Sit here on the sofa until it comes. Are you feeling all right, now?"

He helped her to the sofa and turned to close the door behind him. She heard the lock click and knew she could do nothing about her situation.

Tears coursed down her cheeks as she thought about her parents. She knew she was not in any immediate danger, but they would not know. How they must have worried when she did not get home at three. It was four now, and her mother was probably calling to locate her. *Would they find her car? What about the dinner her parents had planned for the evening at Riverside?* She was far from Riverside now. They had driven in the opposite direction, she was sure. All she could do now was put this in the hands of the One her parents had always put their trust in, and had taught her to turn to -- God.

"Dear God, please comfort my parents. Help me to know what Your will is in this predicament I am in. I am so afraid. I know You are with me and will never leave me. Thank you for the peace You are giving me. Lord, let me be brave." Tears dripped to her sleeve as she sat quietly for a moment.

CHAPTER FOUR

The Marrow household, which was normally full of life, had taken on a feeling of solemnity as Julia and Andrew waited for the phone to ring or the sound of a Toyota to drive into the garage, hoping that still Annie would show up and tell them what had delayed her. They could imagine one of Annie's long-lost friends showing up to surprise her on her birthday and sweeping her away making it impossible for her to have control of the situation.

Those things did happen, didn't they? The hall clock struck five o'clock, and the sun had disappeared; darkness was shrouding the lawn as Julia stepped to the window. No sight of Annie's blue Toyota. Fear gripped Julia, a fear like she had never known.

"Oh, Andrew," she cried. "Where could she be?" Unable to keep the tears back, Julia shook with uncontrollable grief.

Andrew, pulling her close, and with all that was in him, tried to comfort his wife.

"I wish I could answer that in truth, Julia. I am just as worried as you are. I know men are supposed to be a tower of strength at all times and certainly not shed tears, but I ache for the truth and for you and Annie, as well as myself. Honey, I wish and pray that soon I can answer your question."

Andrew held Julia for a long time.

"Andrew, this is such a trivial thought, but what are we going to do about our reservations at Riverside? I can't bear to go without her. Then there are the guests. In less than two hours, we were to be seated. Maybe Annie will rush in at any moment, but what if she doesn't?" Julia looked into Andrew's tired eyes with anxiety.

"You're right, Julia, I feel we must notify the restaurant that possibly there will be no party. They have every right to know the predicament we are in at the time. I'll call Peter Brant, the owner, and ask him to advise me and also ask him to avoid letting the news get around. When I phoned the authorities, they advised that we keep the news from the press, as this could alert anyone who may have taken Annie, even though they do not get alarmed until the person has been missing for twenty-four hours. I'm sure that is procedure today because so many people just run away from their problems, thinking that is the solution. We know that Annie would not do that because she has always worked through her difficulties, and, as far as I know, she is not in any crisis at the moment."

Andrew did not say what came to his mind . . . that a lot could happen in twenty-four hours. He knew this would only add to Julia's suspicion that Annie was in danger.

Andrew went into the study to telephone the restaurant. Julia slumped to the sofa in the den and wept. It seemed to help to cry. Perhaps the grief needed venting.

"I spoke with Peter, Julia. He was so understanding and expressed his compassion in the crisis." Andrew assured her. "I told him that I knew much of the food had been prepared already, and we would take care of the bill whatever. The cake had arrived a few minutes ago. He reminded me that Annie could still come in and if she did, just to give him a ring. I suppose we better call Christina and Katie. I feel that they will help get the news to the others, but please caution them to keep the news in the circle of friends."

Julia's legs trembled as she walked to the phone to dial. She would ring Christina first then Katie. Her heart was heavy as she dialed Christina's number. The phone was ringing . . .

"Is this Mrs. Dodson?" Julia asked. "This is Julia Marrow, could I please speak with Christina?" Julia and Anise Dodson had met at church on one or two occasions but had never really gotten acquainted. Anise was a career mother and out of town often. Her businesslike manner was evident in the way she spoke to Christina.

"Mrs. Marrow, is there something wrong?" Christina asked.

"Yes, Christina, something is definitely wrong. I need your help. I . . . . ," Julia's voice faltered.

"What is it, Mrs. Marrow?" Christina became excited, and her shrill voice brought Julia to her task.

"Christina, you haven't seen . . . A--Annie since this morning, have you?" Julia managed to ask.

"No, I spoke to you, remember, but I haven't seen her since then. Do you mean Annie hasn't come home all day?" Christina was afraid at this news.

"No, Christina, and we have been advised to keep it quiet. Andrew and I thought that she would be driving in at any moment, and she very well could, yet, you know Annie and her punctuality. Honey, we feel we must get word to all the friends that were invited to have dinner at Riverside." Julia felt she could not go on.

"Of course, Mrs. Marrow, I'll call Katie and we will take care of that. Please don't worry about our letting the word out. You're right; it could cause problems if Annie has been taken. But why would anyone abduct Annie? Please, Mrs. Marrow, tell Mr. Marrow that we love both of you so much. I'll hang up now and get the message out. I'll be over just as soon as possible. I love you." Christina could hardly stay brave long enough to hang up the phone. Tears were filling her eyes and affecting her speech.

Julia sat for a long time, she was unaware just how long, trying to make some sense of the day. Andrew had gone out to feed Rover. Men deal with tragedy in a different manner than women, she thought, but the hurt they experience is just as great.

It took her a long time after she married Andrew to realize that he would not react to situations in the same manner she always had been accustomed to reacting. They had experienced a lot in the twenty-four years they had been together as husband and wife. Annie coming into their life had been one of the greatest events and blessings of which they could think.

She and Andrew had both been Christians when they met. They had dreamed how wonderful life would be as they spent time having their daily devotions together before they were married.

They looked forward each day to reading God's Word and praying together. Julia smiled as she thought about reading to Annie as an infant from the Bible. Annie grew up loving the Bible and was taught early in life to go to God with everything.

Julia was reminded of the time Annie so wanted to see snow. It was already mid-December, and there had been very little snowfall in Watertown that year. Meteorologists were predicting an unusual "green" Christmas, but Annie faithfully prayed as a five-year-old that it would snow. It did. Three feet fell and blanketed the whole town. The snowmobilers and skiers were elated. Annie would pray now, she thought. It was consoling to know she not only knew how, but that Annie knew the power of God in her life.

Andrew had said Annie's New Testament was on the seat of her car. She hardly went anywhere without it. *Did this mean she was unexpectedly taken?* Julia knew her thoughts were causing her to fear. *What had the scripture said about fear . . . that it did not come from God.* She must remember that Jesus was with Annie now and would have His will in whatever happened.

Julia had not taken Annie's dress up to her room. She must do this now. The shimmering chiffon of royal blue fell so light as she went into Annie's bedroom. She had left her room so neat.

The fragrance of her cologne lingered, giving a feeling of her presence. Her Bible lay on the nightstand where she had read it last. Julia hung the dress in the closet and turned to leave as Andrew stepped to her side. Julia could taste the tears from her own eyes.

Taking hold of her hand, Andrew led her to Annie's bed and, picking up her Bible, he turned to First Peter 5 and read from verse 7 " . . . casting all your care upon Him, for He cares for you. Be sober, be vigilant; because your adversary the devil walks about like a roaring lion, seeking whom he may devour. Whom resist steadfast in the faith, knowing that the same afflictions are accomplished in your brethren that are in the world. But the God of all grace, who hath called us unto his eternal glory by Christ Jesus, after that ye have suffered a while, make you perfect, stablish, strengthen, settle you. To him be glory and dominion forever and ever. Amen."

CHAPTER FIVE

The lawn at the back of the Manor was well kept, and even though the grass was fading another crop was beginning to appear. Someone had spent time caring for this lovely estate.

The trees swayed in the gentle breeze, and with each movement leaves would turn loose to float to the ground. There had been enough cold weather to make the change from summer to fall, although the day was pleasant with Annie's light jacket and wool skirt. Annie had pulled a chair up, as her knees were shaking, so that she could look out on the landscape. She was reminded of her own window that looked out on her backyard at home. *Was it just this morning that she had stood and visualized sketches of her childhood from her window?* She could almost see a little girl swinging on the rope and board swing that her father had made for her. He would push her, and she would beg to go higher and higher.

What was her father doing now? What would he do about the plans of Dr. Ramsey? Would Ramsey reveal himself or would he just try to keep the center from being built by distracting her father until the building permit ran out? She remembered her father saying something about the fact that their permit was in effect for a limited number of days, and if construction had not started by a certain date, ownership of the land that had been donated for the Good Shepherd Home for Women would revert back to the original heirs. That was the reason her father had to work nights. Delays caused by the typical red tape of New York government, severe weather, lack of funds and various other problems had put off ground breaking until the last minute. Construction was scheduled to start . . . tomorrow! That's why Ramsey had kidnapped her today! Annie became engrossed in her thoughts and did not hear the lock click and the door swing open behind her. The carpet was so plush footsteps were silenced. The man set the tray on the table at the opposite side of the room and walked stealthily behind Annie, close enough to slip his arms around her waist, holding her in a vise-like grip.

"Stop it!" she demanded, gasping for breath and trying to wrench free of his hands.

"A little spitfire, eeh? My! Jason didn't tell me you were so pretty and looked so gooood!" The man laughed, but Annie did not like his laugh or anything about him.

"Take your hands off me!" she demanded, and jerking away struck him with her elbow.

"Oh, Miss High-and-Mighty, you don't know who you are dealing with, do you?" the man snarled. Annie caught the smell of tobacco and perhaps a slight touch of alcohol on his hot breath.

"You must be Steven. I overheard that he would be up to relieve the man who is called Jason," she replied, still in his grip.

"So do you know Steven, Miss Fancypants? He is quite a lady-charmer," the man commented sarcastically with a touch of malice in his voice.

"Just let me go, whoever you are!" she cried, tears beginning to fill her eyes. I must not let him see me crying, she thought. Guys like this like nothing better than to make girls feel weak. She tried to break his hold.

"Louis! Take your hands off the young lady!" a voice from the doorway ordered. "Ramsey warned you not to harm the girl."

Louis dropped his hands as he turned to look in the direction of the voice.

"I wasn't harming her, Jason; she really liked it. She thought I was Steven at first. You know what charm he has with the women, the handsome hunk," Louis turned to look at Annie who was rubbing her arms as if trying to erase his touch.

"She is just pretending with you, Jason. She was different before she sensed you at the door." Louis was smiling a wicked smile at Annie.

She looked across at Jason with fear and lowered her lashes to avoid the tears from streaming down her cheeks.

"Did you tell her about her food, Louis? She has not eaten since morning. I suppose she is very hungry," Jason said, looking from Louis to Annie.

Was that concern in his eyes? She pondered.

"Sit down and eat your meal before it gets cold," Jason said before turning to Louis. "Come outside, Louis. Miss Marrow might prefer to eat alone."

Louis followed Jason out the door and pulled the door shut behind him. The lock clicked after his departure.

Annie looked at the food that was brought on a heavy silver tray. There was baked chicken with potatoes and green beans, a fruit salad for dessert and iced tea. It looked good and she was hungry. Annie took a bite of the chicken. It was delicious and so tender. The beans had the taste of fried bacon, she remembered the smell of bacon that her mother had prepared for her very special birthday breakfast. With this, her appetite was gone.

What was her mother doing now? Three o'clock was two hours ago, and in two more hours she was due to go with her parents to Riverside for her birthday celebration. Today had started out such a happy day until . . . *Oh, how could I have been so stupid? I was so dumb to accept this man without asking questions.* Tears were dripping in her meal, and her stomach felt that the food already there was going to come up. She set the tray on the table and curled up on one end of the sofa.

What could she do? Was there a way to escape? And this Louis -- she did not like him one bit. He reminded her of a boy Cathy Sams had dated at one time. He treated girls like they were put here just for him and forced himself on them by touching them constantly even though they let him know his advances were not wanted. Cathy left their circle and stopped coming to church because she knew we avoided Eddie. Louis is like Eddie.

What had Jason said? That she would be guarded, or did he say something else like "your guards, or shall I say your companions, will be Steven, Louis and myself." She had not been so afraid in the presence of Jason, but Louis was another story.

I must stop thinking about him and put some constructive thoughts in my mind, she said to herself. *Dad always said when fear came, to think of one of the verses that I had memorized that gave me power over fear.* She began to think. . . . God is not the author of fear. So if He wasn't, that only means the devil is, she reasoned. "I will fear no evil for Thou art with me."

Yes, the verse from the twenty-third Psalm. You ARE with me. Jesus is with me at this very minute and will be with me even when Louis comes into my room.

"Oh, Jesus, let me know the power of Your presence over this feeling of fear," Annie whispered.

The lock clicked and the door opened. Annie looked up, reluctantly, through her dark long lashes. Louis had returned to the suite. He was looking at the tray of food that except for a few bites looked almost as it did when he left it before going out the door with Jason.

"So, Miss High-and-Mighty did not like the food we brought her," he sneered at her.

"The food was very good, but I seemed to be full after a few bites.

Thank you for bringing it to me . . . I had been so hungry," she replied, avoiding his dark eyes on her.

"Well, now, you seem almost human. Could it be you have been thinking about me and all my charms?" He laughed a cold, calculating laugh.

"I have been thinking about how nice you could be if you wanted to be nice," she answered with the nervousness she was feeling hidden in her voice.

"You don't think I am very nice. I've never been told that by any other female. They usually like the way I treat them." He came closer to the sofa with a gleam of conceit in his eyes.

"Perhaps the girls you have met see you differently than I do," Annie said without looking at him. It was better that she not look at the enemy and keep in the direction of her strategy.

"And just how do you see me, my lovely lady?" He was getting angry, by the tone of his voice.

"I see you depending on yourself and what you call your charm with people to get you what you want," she said getting closer to sharing the truth with him. He needed someone to tell him about his problem, but she was wondering if she was going to have the courage.

At that particular moment Louis remembered the tray needed to go back to the kitchen. Suppose she tried to use something off that tray to escape. He turned to pick it up, and as he opened the door, he remarked with his white teeth showing behind his dark mustache and his eyes boring into her thoughts, "I will be back shortly to use some of that charm on you, Miss Marrow."

The door closed and the lock turned. Annie could barely hear footsteps outside the door. He could be a good-looking man, maybe not considered handsome, but good-looking. He appeared so confident, but that could be a cover for insecurity. She needed to watch her step with him; Jason might not be in the house or at least near enough next time.

As there was nothing to turn to in the way of keeping herself entertained, no television, no magazines, and since she had left her New Testament in the car, she would have to recall all the verses and songs she could to keep sane. At least the suite was nice. Her mind turned to the story about Paul and Silas . . . they were held in a dungeon. That would be horrible for her as she hated darkness and feared crawling things. She had never been one to bait her hook when she went fishing because she hated the wiggly worms her father often used for bait.

No, she still had something to be thankful for and she must remember that. *Thank you, Jesus, that I'm not in a dungeon. What did the scripture say that Paul and Silas did while in prison? They were singing.* Annie loved to sing.

She began to sing "I must tell Jesus, I must tell Jesus, I cannot bear this burden alone. I must tell Jesus, I must tell Jesus, Jesus will help me. Jesus alone." The melody rang through her mind after she had sung the words and she continued to hum it.

It is funny, Annie thought, how just singing those words can make me feel close to Jesus. If it were not for Louis, she felt she would not be so despondent. She watched the hands of her watch as they moved closer and closer to seven o"clock. The birthday dinner. How she hated that her parents had to be put through this worry.

She wished she could tell them that she was safe . . . as safe as a girl could be held captive by someone like Louis. How she disliked him. Her father had always told her that even though we might not like someone, Jesus died for that person just the same. *I imagine Paul and Silas did not especially care for the jailor who had them chained in stocks, but they led him to Jesus.*

Could it be that Louis just doesn't know Jesus? Perhaps he has heard about Him. Almost everyone in the States has heard of Him. But his eyes are blind to the goodness of God. He would be hard to convince.

But, was she to convince him of God's goodness or show it in her life and let the Holy Spirit convince him of his need for God's mercy? A tear dropped on her grey wool skirt as she thought about the safety of home and family. She prayed that her father would somehow know that she wanted him to continue in his plans for the center. She remembered overhearing him say that if construction did not start tomorrow as planned, the heirs would receive back the donated land, and the Good Shepherd Home for Women would be only a dream of the past.

Oh, God, don't let him be hindered in his work for You. He was so sure that this center would reach a lot of girls and provide help in the way of housing, clothes and food, as well as care of physicians and hospital care during their pregnancies. Then those who chose to give their little babies up for adoption could work through the agency to place them in good Christian homes. Many girls had been reached through the resource facility already there. *How I wish I could tell him to go ahead with his work.*

Dr. Ramsey had said he meant her no harm. Could he be trusted? Was he blind to what he was really doing through abortion? *Even though he seems cold and calculating, does he have a soft spot somewhere that has not been touched?* Her mother had always told her that people we give up on, God still works with. We are so human; we see people's lives as hopeless, but God sees His power.

Annie heard the rattle of the lock, and suddenly the door opened. Louis swaggered in and sat by her on the sofa. It was all she could do to remain calm, but she must if she was to help him in any way.

Annie began to hum a song she had sung in church many times . . . "What a friend we have in Jesus . . ." A smile was on her face in the presence of fear.

"You must be a fanatic," Louis retorted. "Singing and humming those church songs."

"Why would that make me a fanatic?" she asked calmly.

"Most people who go around singing and humming religious songs think God can do anything."

"No, Louis, I agree there are people who appear to be fanatical about certain religious beliefs and activities, but there are those who are dependent upon God. Yes, we make mistakes at times and are not perfect but we recognize God as sovereign. He can do all things, if it is His will and time."

Annie could not believe she had been so bold.

"And you are one of those goody-goody trusting people." He sounded angry. "Tell me how your God is going to protect you tonight from me. I am going to be here all night. Does that not make you afraid?" He laughed at his threat.

"Are you trying to make me afraid, Louis?" she asked.

"I just want you to know that whatever I choose to do with you, I will. If that makes you afraid." He stood up and came to peer down at her.

Annie did not look up but sighed a long sigh. Perhaps she should stop talking now and concentrate on what the night had in store for her. She knew she could not sleep, even though she was drained emotionally from the events of the day.

Louis walked to the window and looked out into the night. This girl was different. She was sure pretty, too. Ramsey had warned him about his behavior with her; even Ramsey recognized that she was special.

Louis turned and walked to the door. He needed some fresh air. He took the key from his pocket and opened the door. He walked out without a word to Annie.

Annie listened for the lock. She did not hear it. She would give him a few minutes and see what happened. Was this her chance to escape? Should she get out of the room? Where would she go? . . . Yet, this may be her only chance. If she failed to give it a try, she would always wonder if she could have made it.

Walking softly to the door, her heart pounding so loudly that she was sure someone could hear, she turned the knob and stepped into the corridor. She looked over the balcony . . . . No one was in sight.

Should she risk going past the closed door and to the top of the stairs?

She wished her heart would stop pounding so loudly; the house was so quiet. She must be the only person there besides Louis . . . that brought more anxiety to her mind. She took a couple of steps toward the top of the stairs. . . . .

CHAPTER SIX

The doorbell rang just as the clock in the foyer struck seven. Julia and Andrew came down the stairs reluctantly. At the bottom of the stairs, Andrew rushed to the door. There stood Christina and Nathan.

"Mr. Marrow, we hope you won't mind our coming over. We felt you needed us, and we certainly needed you and Mrs. Marrow," Nathan said with a note of sadness.

"Of course, we don't mind. Please come on in. Are the other kids with you?" Andrew asked looking toward the street at the car.

"Well, yes sir, Katie and Tony wanted to come with us," Nathan replied.

"Katie, Tony, come on in," Andrew invited. "We are always happy to have Annie's friends spend time with us, and especially tonight."

Julia came forward to greet the group. Christina hugged her and led her into the den. Katie followed them. Nathan slipped his arm around Andrew's shoulder, and along with Tony they followed the other three.

"Please sit down," Julia said as she moved cushions from the sofa to make room.

"Have you had dinner already?" Andrew asked, taking in the group.

"Well, we weren't that hungry and decided to wait until later," Nathan answered for the group.

"We found ourselves in the same condition," Julia said as she kept her eyes lowered so the tears would not show. "You must need something to drink. I'll go out to the kitchen and get us all something."

"Oh, please let Katie and me do it," Christina said enthusiastically, feeling that was one way the two of them could help. "Would everyone take coffee?"

"Are you making it?" Nathan teased. Christina gave him a peck on the shoulder.

It just dawned on Julia that she had not inquired about the other guests that were invited to the dinner. How she hated to think of that.

"Did you reach all the guests with our message?" Julia asked.

"Oh, yes, Mrs. Marrow, we did, and everyone wanted to come over, but we felt that would be too overwhelming. They agreed to drop in later, but they wanted you to know that you were in their thoughts and prayers," Katie said and put her hand on Mrs. Marrow's before she left the sofa to go into the kitchen with Christina.

"Mr. Marrow," Nathan began and dropped his head before he could go on, "I guess from what we can determine, I was one of the last people to see Annie before she . . . , that is, as she left school."

"Did you see her with anyone?" Mr. Marrow asked intently.

"No, I was trying to find Christina to go to lunch with me, and Annie and I met in the hall. We only spoke briefly. She seemed to be in a hurry. Later Christina told me she had some errands to run and had to pick up her dress for the dinner."

Tony sat quietly, listening to the conversation. He felt that he had so little to contribute. He had been trying to get Annie to go out with him. He had dated her on a few occasions, and they had had some good times together. He could see her as she looked the last time he came to pick her up for dinner. She was so full of life. Her eyes seemed to glow as she came down the stairs. The blue dress she wore was the color of her eyes. He remembered that he and Mr. Marrow were standing at the foot of the stairs; she kissed her father on the cheek and went in search of her mother before they left. They had driven to a little steakhouse in a town twenty miles away. Annie had talked about her classes at the college. He thought how excited she was to begin work on her degree in elementary education. She then told him about her father's work with the pregnancy resource center and his vision for the pregnancy care center and adoption home.

She had helped in the resource center after school and was surprised at the many girls who came for help. She had been undecided about whether she wanted to get a degree in education or go into counseling. They had agreed that the first two years were basic courses, and even if she wanted to change later, she could do so.

Was Mr. Marrow speaking to him? . . . As in a trance, Tony looked at Annie's father.

"I was inquiring about your work, Tony. I understand that you are a new physician at the Good Samaritan Hospital."

"Yes, I am. I am finding my work very interesting. I believe I have chosen well. There have been times through the past seven years that I was not sure that I was suited to become a physician. I guess that happens to you whatever vocation you choose. I have found my work more important since I became a Christian."

"I think of Dr. Luke as a prime example of a New Testament Christian," Mr. Marrow said and smiled at Tony. He thought what a fine young man this Tony was. He wondered how Annie really felt about him. Oh, if only he knew where she was and if she was safe.

His eyes took on a dreaminess, unseeing.

"What did the authorities say about Annie's disappearance, Mr. Marrow?" Nathan asked as he sat on the edge of his chair with his elbows on his knees and leaned forward intently.

"You know, they do not consider one missing until they have been gone twenty-four hours. They advised us to wait and keep quiet about it so the papers and media would not get wind of it," Mr. Marrow looked with worry in his eyes.

"I checked with all the local clinics and hospitals in the area, even in Syracuse," Tony offered. "I do hope you do not think me assuming too much in doing so. I felt, in my position, I could do it without suspicion."

"No, Tony," Mr. Marrow replied and put his hand on Tony's shoulder. "Thank you, son. We appreciate all the help we can get."

At this point the girls returned with coffee and served the Marrows and then Nathan and Tony.

Nathan watched as Mrs. Marrow hardly touched her coffee. These were two people of all the people who deserved this tragedy least. They had always helped others. He remembered when he first started attending New Hope Community Church; they had been so encouraging to him. They were always inviting a group into their home, serving cookies and sodas, and Mr. Marrow would always get some game going. They would laugh at his antics. He was so much fun.

Mrs. Marrow made everyone feel at home bringing in cookies and laughing her merry little laugh. Of course, Annie was in her element when she had her friends around. She was such a sharing person. She seemed to look at her friends as the brothers and sisters she did not have. Many times he remembered little children being in the home. They were included just as if they were going to be there always. But of all the things that stood out in his memory was the family's devotion to Christ. Before they would leave the house, Mr. Marrow would call them into the den and ask them to all sit down wherever they could, sometimes on the floor if necessary, and he would share just one verse. He would say, "This was my verse God gave me today. I want to give it to you." He would read or say the verse; then either he would pray or Mrs. Marrow would. Nathan remembered one time when he was asked to pray. He felt it was a great privilege because Mr. Marrow made it such an important part of his life.

This is where the two of them are drawing strength, Nathan thought. *They know God in a personal way and are trusting Him with Annie. They are clinging to God's promises.*

Christina broke in on Nathan's thoughts as she said, "Nathan, do you think we could go pick up something to eat? Mr. and Mrs. Marrow will need something, and I am sure Mrs. Marrow did not cook today."

"Of course," Nathan said. "That's a great idea. Too bad I did not think of it since I have such a great mind." This brought a chuckle from Annie's parents as they saw Nathan using his wonderful ability to be humorous.

"Tony and I will set the table and put the ice in the glasses while you are gone." Katie turned to Tony and beckoned him to join her.

"Before you go, Nathan and Christina, could we just gather here in the den, as we have so many times before, and join in communing with God?" Andrew asked. "Your idea to pick up dinner is a good one, but I think we need to spend a little moment with One Who knows the plans he has for someone we all love. You know He is not looking at Annie as a person who has disappeared or a missing person. He knows exactly where she is. I want to share a verse with you that has comforted me." He began to read the verse and he put his arm around his wife, drawing her head on his shoulder.

"'Thou knowest my downsitting and my uprising, Thou understandest my thought afar off. Thou compasseth my path and my lying down, and art acquainted with all my ways.'

"David wanted to tell us about God. God inspired him to write this, and tonight God has made us a promise that He knows where Annie is. He is aware of her sitting down and rising up. He is aware of the thoughts she has and of our thoughts. He knows the paths she will walk, and where she is lying down tonight. He knows all her ways and this gives me strength."

CHAPTER SEVEN

Suddenly the door of the room to her left opened; she was directly in front of it. Hard cold hands grabbed her, and with one hand over her mouth, the man dragged her toward the room she had just left. Pushing the door open, he shoved her inside the room with so much force she almost lost her footing.

"You little sneak! You goody-two-shoes! You are no different from all the others. Turn your back on you and you try something. Did you not know I was playing cat and mouse with you?" Louis was so close to her, binding her arms to her back.

"Don't you ever try that again! Now, you have really made me mad! Do you understand?" He pushed her down on the sofa with vengeance.

Annie did not know what to expect from him. His eyes were wild with anger as he stood over her glaring. She felt terrified. If she had planned to sleep tonight, that was out of the question now.

"I was planning to leave you to yourself tonight so you would get some sleep. Now I will be here!" Louis glared at her.

What should she do now? She had failed to escape. Had she been foolish to try? She seemed to be just asking for more trouble in what she had just done. She decided to change her strategy.

She looked up at the hard angry eyes of her captor.

"How would you feel, held captive by strangers?" she asked. "Would you not try to escape if given a slight chance?"

"Did you think I would be so stupid to let you get away?" he questioned. "What do you take me for anyway? You haven't listened to a word I've said, have you?" He looked at her with malice in his eyes.

"I did the only thing I could think of when I did not hear the lock click when you left. I don't want to stay here. My parents are worried sick about me. I don't know you, and this is such an injustice."

"Don't you think it is an injustice for your father to try to tell these girls that they are killing a baby when they have an abortion? Don't you and your father know that could upset them?"

He was standing over her, and she thought about him. *Was he perhaps the father of some of those unborn children who had been aborted at the clinic?*

"I think it's an injustice if these girls are not allowed to hear the truth about abortions," Annie declared. "The Bible says in Psalms: 'For Thou hast possessed my reins; Thou hast covered me in my mother's womb. I will praise Thee, for I am fearfully and wonderfully made. My substance was not hid from Thee, when I was made in secret, and curiously wrought in the lowest parts of the earth. Thine eyes did see my substance yet being imperfect and in Thy book, all my members were written.'

"As that unborn is formed, God is forming a human being. Perhaps He has a great work for that unborn baby to do when he is an adult. I believe every girl should hear that truth . . . not that this is just a mass of tissue but that God is particular in forming a child. Is that too much to ask?" she declared in boldness.

Louis had moved away from her, and when he turned around he was angry.

"You think you are so smart, spouting all your Bible verses!"

Annie had stood up and walked to the window. All was dark on the lawn. She was here all alone with this stranger. The old fear became evident again.

Suddenly Louis's arms were around her. Annie began pushing him with all her might. He whispered in her ear, "Didn't the Bible say also that woman was to be submissive to man?"

He breathed heavily in her ear. He was trying to kiss her as she fought him off.

"Stop, Louis!" she yelled. "Please stop!"

As if afraid someone would hear her, he released his hold on her. She ran to the other side of the room. Would she be able to lock the bedroom and keep him out? She wondered. Making a break for the bedroom, she closed the door and locked it.

"Miss Marrow, you are not running away from me by dodging into the bedroom. My key also fits that lock." His laughter brought tears to her eyes. She sat quietly for a few moments, afraid she would go to sleep, and began to recite every scripture verse that came to her mind.

How would she ever get through this night? She wondered, realizing she would fall asleep from exhaustion.

"I must stay awake," Annie whispered to herself. "I must." Her eyes were heavy and her head ached from not eating properly. *If I stay still I will surely go to sleep*, she reminded herself.

This line of thinking brought her to her feet. She walked around in the bedroom. She moved over to the window. The blinds had not been drawn. They were open as they had been when she arrived. She looked out over the lawn.

There were lights along the stream at the back; they glimmered in the water. *This could be a beautiful place if I were under any other circumstances*, she mused. *What was Louis doing?* She could not hear him moving on the plush carpet of the sitting room. He was so angry with her, she feared his reaction.

Did he really have a key to her bedroom? Not knowing the answer meant she must keep her eyes open. She continued to walk around in the room. She went into the bathroom, and turning the water on she splashed her face.

The water was cold. Perhaps that would help her to stay awake. She looked around at the shiny white fixtures, so clean and the expensive embroidered towels that hung on the brass towel holder. How good it would feel to sink into a tub of warm water. She picked up a bottle on the brass stand near the tub . . . bubble bath. Unscrewing the top, she could smell the fragrance as it filled the room. She did not recognize the label or the fragrance, obviously a costly item.

She rubbed her hands over the fluffy bath towels and hugged them to her as if they were a teddy bear. When she was a little girl she had a teddy bear that had been a comfort when she was afraid. She and Teddy had weathered many storms.

What was that noise? A knock on her door? Oh, no, was it Louis? She returned to the bedroom, her pulse began to beat rapidly and she experienced a smothering sensation in her throat.

"Did you hear me in there, Goody-two-shoes?" Louis asked as he knocked on the door. "Why don't you come out and keep me company? It's going to be a long night, and I don't like spending it alone."

Should she pretend to be asleep? She kept quiet and waited.

"Did you hear me, Miss Marrow, or will I have to come in there and keep you company?" He chuckled. "That sounds like a better idea." She heard a key in the lock.

"No, I'll be out in a minute," she answered. She thought she would prefer spending time with Louis, in his frame of mind, in the sitting room rather than the bedroom. He was so repulsive to her in this mood.

Running the gold comb from the comb and brush set on the cabinet though her blonde curls until they looked like pulled taffy, she walked to the door, with a prayer in her heart. She listened at the door. Would

45

she collide with Louis if she opened the door? She turned the knob and opened the door. Louis was seated in a wingback chair beside the fireplace. She walked to the sofa and sat as far away from him as she could. She kept her eyes lowered, fearing to meet his dark ones.

"That's better," he said and smiled a crooked smile at her. "I see you tidied up your curls. Did you do that to impress me?" He laughed, making her uncomfortable.

Annie had read of a woman who had been taken hostage, and her life was threatened. *I am not threatened with my life,* she thought, *but this other threat is just as frightening.*

"What do you Christians do for excitement, Goody-two-shoes?" he asked not because he was interested, she knew, but to taunt her.

"Do you really want to know, Louis, or do you think you can anger me by asking?" she said calmly.

"I have known some of your kind before who were no different from anyone else. I am guessing you would be just the same."

He looked at her with vileness in his eyes.

"I will admit, many Christians do not draw on the power that is within them to keep their lives pure, but I choose to remain pure and live so that I have nothing for which to be ashamed," Annie said in a sweet calm voice.

"What if you don't have a choice in the matter? I have already shown you, Miss Marrow, that if I choose I could do what I wanted with you." He stood up and moved to the sofa.

Annie, sensing his move, went behind the sofa, putting the sofa between them. She would not let him see the fear she was experiencing.

"You told me you wanted us to keep each other company. It was my assumption that we could talk and even that there was a chance we would find a common ground of communication," she informed him, trying to keep her voice from trembling. Was she asking for trouble? Should she have remained in her bedroom? *Perhaps his key would not fit that lock, but he had said it would.*

Before Annie could realize what was happening, Louis reached back and caught her hands in his big hard hands and pulled her against him. Annie, weak from lack of food and loss of sleep, fought with all her might to get out of his grasp, but to no avail. Louis began to laugh.

"Where is that power, now, Goody-two-shoes? Did I not tell you that whatever I wanted I got?"

His hold on her was impossible to break, and Annie, fearing the worst and still resisting his embrace, felt the hot tears on her cheeks. The only defense she had was to do as the woman she had read about did. She could feel Louis's lips on her cheek.

"Jesus," she said. "Please help Louis understand the way I feel."

Louis began to laugh, yet he still held her. "Goody-two-shoes, do you think that will scare me off?" he asked, his hot breath on her face. "I am not afraid of your Jesus."

At that moment a knock sounded at the door. Another knock, and then someone was pounding at the door. Louis, fearing that it could be Dr. Ramsey, released Annie and turned to the door. The key turned and bursting into the room was an auburn-haired girl about the size of Annie. She wore jeans that were a size too small and a very tight sweater of turquoise. Her eyes were blazing with anger as she looked across the room at Annie's tousled blonde curls.

"Who do you think you are?" she stormed at Annie.

"Leave her alone, Darlene!" Louis demanded.

"Is this THE Miss Marrow, who has such a famous father?" Darlene sneered. "Miss Marrow, I advise you to leave Louis alone. He could be too much for little ole you." Darlene laughingly looked up into Louis's eyes.

Annie kept silent, as she did not know what was expected of her in the way of an answer. She would be glad to leave Louis to this girl or any other girl.

"Louis, you know when I am here I like for you to spend time with me," Darlene pleaded.

"I am working tonight, Darlene," he answered her plea.

"Working? working? From the way Miss Marrow looked when I walked in, it didn't appear you were working," Darlene said, turning a coy look on Annie.

Annie could feel the blush covering her face. Should she inform Darlene of the truth or keep her tongue out of this sparring match? She chose to remain silent.

"Louis, can't you lock her door and come next door for a few hours? You can hear, if she tries to escape. Ramsey did not mean you had to stay in her room all the time!" Darlene's hand was on Louis's arm, caressingly.

"Is Ramsey here?" Louis asked.

"Yes, he brought me out after the clinic closed. I helped with the filing today. He has almost promised me a full-time job. Let's go next door, and I'll tell you all about it," she said, convincingly.

"All right, Darlene. Hey, Goody-two-shoes, you better try to sleep. Don't think you can get away from here." He glared at Annie, and then smiled his wicked smile.

He put his key in the lock, and he and Darlene stepped into the corridor. Closing the door, he locked it, and they were gone. Annie felt relief as she assumed Darlene would keep him occupied for a few hours anyway. She decided after a few minutes of silence to go into the bedroom, close the door and lock it. She looked at the sparkling white tub. Did she dare?

If she could get a quick bath, she felt like she would be able to endure the night. She started the water and rushed back to the door to listen for any sign of Louis. She reasoned with herself. *Am I going to allow him to terrorize me all night?*

Turning the water off, she stepped into the tub after laying her clothes so she could reach them. She would put the sweater and skirt back on as she did not want to wear the clothes that had been provided for her even though they were lovely. After a brief stay in the tub, soaping her body with the apricot-scented soap, she let the water out and dried herself off with a nice fluffy towel and slipped back into her own sweater and skirt.

She brushed her teeth with a new brush she found in the cabinet; then brushed her hair until it fell in shimmering curls about her face. Annie sat on the edge of the bed and looked at a magazine she found in the nightstand. The smiling faces of models stared back at a sad-faced girl. She wished she had her New Testament or the Bible on her nightstand at home. She began to say the twenty-third Psalm: "The Lord is my shepherd, I shall not want. He maketh me lie down in green pastures. . . . . and on . . . . . Yea, though I walk through the valley of the shadow of death, I will fear no evil, for Thou . . . . art . . . . with . . . . me . . .

CHAPTER EIGHT

The rain fell noisily on the roof as Julia crawled out of bed. Andrew had left her sleeping as her night had been fitful. Each time she would drop off to sleep, dreams would haunt her with episodes of Annie trying to reach them, waking her with a start. In tears, she would be comforted by her husband.

As Julia dressed, she felt as if lead weights were attached to her feet. Her heart was heavy with grief, and as she looked into the mirror she seemed to be looking into the eyes of a stranger.

Lifting the lid of her makeup kit, she tried to bring her face alive. How could she get though the day without knowing where Annie was? *Why had she been taken, if she had, and what other reason could explain her disappearance?*

Julia started down the stairs, and as her foot touched the top step, she turned to walk back to Annie's room. The house seemed so empty without her.

The comfort of Annie's room seemed to give Julia the feeling of her daughter's presence. Perhaps that is silly, Julia thought.

She picked up Annie's Bible and hugged it to her heart. Annie had received the Bible on her sixteenth birthday, and she cherished it. Julia's hands caressed the blue leather binding as she prayed for her child's safety. The room had Annie's personality -- neat, orderly and everything matching to perfection.

Julia remembered Annie decorating her bedroom with the ivory walls. Annie had spent days picking out each item. The painting of the walls was done by Annie during one of her spring vacations.

Julia rubbed her hands over the soft downy coverlet of pale pink with tiny flowers of deeper pink and willow green leaves. The deep pink dust ruffle matched the flowers to perfection.

"Yes," she whispered, "this room has your personality, honey."

Walking to the window overlooking the backyard, Julia stood where Annie had stood just about twenty-four hours ago and watched the rain as it pelted down. She was in the house alone as Andrew had a meeting with the center's board this morning in order to over- see the start of the construction of the buildings. He had wanted to call the co-chairman to tell him he would be unable to attend, but Julia had insisted that he go on. Julia realized how important this was to Andrew as well as the community. She had reminded him that Annie would have wanted him to go had she been able to tell him herself.

Annie was such an unselfish person. Even as a little girl . . . the memory of Annie when she celebrated her sixth birthday flashed before Julia's mind.

Andrew had promised that he would spend the entire day with her, and they would plant a flower garden in the corner of the yard. They would plant chrysanthemums as this was a flower that could be planted late in the season. Annie woke up all excited that morning and came tumbling into bed with them, her bright blue eyes full of anticipation.

As they were eating breakfast the telephone rang, and they were informed that Social Services had a little boy who needed a home for a few days. Could they give him one as he needed to be placed immediately?

Andrew turned to Annie, explaining that he would need to go to Social Services to pick up Jody, would she mind? He told Annie that Jody's father had been unkind to his mother and to Jody, and he could not stay in his own home safely.

Annie ran to her father and hugged him and exclaimed, "You can be his father for a while and he can be my brother!"

Jody had helped plant the garden.

The sound of the telephone ringing broke into Julia's memory, and she went to the bedside to answer it. So many friends, who had heard it from their church members, had called. They were all praying.

"Hello . . . oh, Pastor Thomason . . . no, there has been no word . . . thank you for coming last night. You and Lori were such a comfort to Andrew and me . . . yes, he has gone to meet with the board. Our only comfort is that Annie is in God's care, wherever she is. Thank you for your prayers. We know the power of prayer . . . yes, I will tell him . . . good-bye."

Julia hung up the receiver.

The clock in the hall was striking eleven when Julia came down the stairs. Going into the kitchen, she poured a cup of coffee and picked up her well-worn Bible. Sitting at the small kitchen table, where each morning they had breakfast as a family when at all possible, she turned to Psalms. David had faced so many problems in his life, and he had left us the evidence of his trust through the Psalms he had been inspired to write. Psalm 61 was the Psalm Julia read this morning.

"'Hear my cry, O God, attend unto my prayer,'" she began. "'I will cry unto Thee, when my heart is overwhelmed: lead me to the rock that is higher than I. Thou hast been a shelter for me, and a strong tower from the enemy. . . . I will trust in the cover of Thy wings . . .'"

"Oh, God, this is my prayer this morning," she prayed. "I need your strength to get through each moment. My heart is also overwhelmed. I need lifting to that rock that is higher than I am. Shelter me. But most of all lift up Annie. Shelter her, Father. Be a strong tower from the enemy for her. Keep her under the protection of Thy wings. In Jesus, Amen."

A car pulled into the driveway, and Andrew rushed in the garage door. He had not liked the idea of leaving Julia alone, but she had insisted he go. He was so uneasy when he was away from the phone. Suppose someone called with word of Annie. . . . He knew Julia was so worried and feared she would not be able to handle any bad news. He checked his thinking. *Nothing bad must happen to Annie. His faith must remain strong. God was taking care of her.*

"Any news?" he asked as he kissed Julia.

"No, only Pastor Thomason called and offered to go with you when you went to the police station today. I told him I would give you the message, and you would be returning his call," Julia offered.

"Yes, I would like his company. Do you suppose Lori could stay with you?" Andrew inquired with concern.

"He said he would drop her by and pick you up in his car," Julia fought back the tears that were trying to fill her eyes.

"Honey, everything is going to be all right. I don't understand, but I believe God will take care of Annie. She has been like a promise in our life. We have brought her up to trust him, and she is so strong in her faith. We have always prayed that God would find glory in her life, and this could be the path to His being glorified through her. Don't ask me how, I don't know, but He does."

Andrew was holding Julia close and stroking her curly honey-colored hair.

"We must trust Him to work it out," he said. "In my devotional time this morning, I was reading the thirty-fourth Psalm, and there are so many verses that gave me a promise of God's protection. I must keep His Word ever before me in this time of affliction," Andrew said as though reminding himself.

"Julia, George Watson said something in our meeting this morning that has some validity to it. I am not sure that it is a lead in this case, but he told me that many of the abortion supporters had been phoning the board members and harassing them about this center that we are planning to open. I guess we have been spared with our unlisted number. He is of the opinion that all this could be the work of the pro-choice movement. In our discussion, we really came to no definite lead, but the Good Shepherd Home for Women has really stirred up a hornet's nest among those at the local Woman's Clinic. I feel I must mention this to the police when I see them today."

Andrew turned to the telephone and dialed.

"Chief Garrison, please." Andrew spoke into the phone. "Yes, . . . oh, good morning, Gregory. Andrew Marrow here . . . yes, I'm afraid she's still missing. Could we come by this afternoon to talk with you? . . . All right, we will see you at three . . . Thank you, Gregory. I appreciate your help." With this, Andrew hung up the phone.

"Andrew, if this speculation is true, what do you think they anticipate that taking Annie could accomplish?" Julia asked, with thoughts running rampant in her mind.

"I'm not sure. Perhaps to keep our minds so on Annie's disappearance that they could accomplish something that we are not aware of. I just don't know, honey," Andrew drew Julia to him and held her hoping to comfort her. He too had many thoughts that he did not think he could share with Julia at the time.

Would they go so far as to . . . no, surely not that.

CHAPTER NINE

Annie's hands clawed and pushed, and forming a fist, she pounded the person bending over her.

"Stop it! Stop it!" she screamed, turning her head from one side to the other, hoping to avoid the advances of the man. She kept pounding the hard chest and kicking her legs as if she could run away.

"Louis, stop, you brute!" Her eyes were closed as if she were in a nightmare. Someone was shaking her. She opened her eyes and found she was making eye contact with, not the dark eyes of Louis, but the bluest eyes she had ever seen. They were the color of London blue topaz and fringed with long dark lashes that seemed to have been curled to perfection. The hands that were warding off her blows were gentle yet firm, and she thought this was the most handsome man she had ever seen.

"Well, you are a little spitfire," the perfectly shaped mouth said with a slight grin playing at the corners. "Did you have a bad experience with Louis?" he asked. "He sometimes has difficulty with the women, especially the good-looking ones."

"W . . . Who are you?" Annie finally got the words out.

"Steven Billups," he answered, still holding her arms.

"Please let me go," Annie said with defiance in her voice.

"Only if you promise not to make me the target of your frustrated little fists," he said laughingly.

Immediately his hold on her arms was released, and he backed away from the bed. Annie swung her legs to the side and found the floor with her feet. She made an attempt to rise but swayed. Steven stepped toward her as if to catch her if she were to fall.

Annie caught the head of the bed and steadied herself without acknowledging his attempt to help.

"Well, Mr. Billups, are you my new guard?" she looked directly at the man as she inquired.

"I'm afraid so, Miss Marrow," he answered, still observing her in case she should lose her balance. "When have you eaten?" he asked with a touch of concern in his voice.

"I am a little hungry," Annie said, as if to herself. "How did you get into the bedroom?" She turned angry inquiring eyes on him.

"I just came up to the suite and after listening at the door of your bedroom, found all was silent. I waited until after ten o'clock and still silence. I was beginning to think you had escaped, so I turned the knob, and the door swung open. You were lying there so still and silent, I thought I had better see if you were breathing. That is when I bent over you to check, and you began to attack me as if I were Jack the Ripper.

"You kept pounding my chest, and then I caught hold of your arms trying to calm you, but you acted as if you felt I was going to take advantage of you. You were yelling at Louis."

He looked at her with concern. She was such a delicate little thing. She had probably been protected from guys like Louis. *Why had Ramsey put him with her to guard her, knowing his reputation? Was he using Louis to put fear in her heart and dissuade her from having ideas of escape, as if she could?*

Annie seemed to vaguely remember in her fitful night going to the door to listen for Louis. She could have opened the door without being aware of it.

"Did Louis harm you in any way?" he felt he must ask.

"No," she answered, without looking at him.

"Listen, why don't you let me go down for your breakfast while you tidy up," he suggested with almost tenderness in his voice.

"Whatever you say," Annie said in a whisper almost absently. Somehow she felt safe with Steven Billups. He seemed actually decent. *How had he gotten involved in this kind of underhanded arrangement? Was he just as bad as Louis, yet a wolf dressed in sheep's clothing?*

"I'll be back shortly," Steven said as he closed the door behind him and crossed to the sitting room door. She heard the lock as he made sure she did not escape.

Did Steven know how serious this was? Kidnapping? He was a grown man. Probably in his late twenties or early thirties. He had the most beautiful eyes Annie had ever seen. He was really a very handsome man, she thought. The blue cable knit sweater of soft cotton brought out the vivid blue of his perfectly almond shaped eyes. What had Louis said about his charm with the women and being a handsome hunk? He certainly was that, Annie thought as she turned the water on and began splashing it on her face.

Looking in the mirror, she saw someone who seemed a stranger to her. Dark circles hung around her eyes that had seemingly lost their luster. Her hair was tousled, and her clothes looked like she had worn them for weeks. If she was kept here very long, she would be forced to wear the clothes that had been provided for her even though she was rebelling against the thought. Well, she would worry about that when she had to.

Now, to make herself look alive enough to face breakfast. She ran the comb through her hair, causing it to gleam with golden highlights as it fell on her shoulder. She wished she had something to tie it up with. Oh, well, she would not think about that either. She smoothed down her skirt and straightened her sweater. She slipped her feet into her hose and stepped into her shoes.

Should she make her bed? This was such a part of her routine each day to keep the house tidy that she started to pull the comforter up. She heard the key in the outer door.

"Breakfast is served, Miss Marrow," a gentle voice announced.

Annie stepped into the sitting room and unaware of the effect her appearance had on Steven Billups, she walked to the chair beside the table where he had just placed the large silver tray.

Her eyes were downcast as she looked under the cover to find a full course breakfast — ham, eggs, hashbrowns, toast, and juice, and a sweetroll filled with raspberries. Coffee in a silver server sat beside the elaborate meal. She sat there for a moment before she bowed her head and thanked God for the food.

Steven came forward as soon as she lifted her head and, picking up the silver service, poured her a steaming cup of coffee in the cream-colored cup embellished with pale pink apple blossoms.

Annie looked up to find his eyes and, glancing away, she said in almost a whisper, "Thank you, Mr. Billups."

"Don't you think you can call me Steven? You called Louis, Louis, and Jason, Jason," he said smiling at her. She would not look directly at him.

What is wrong? Steven questioned in his mind. *Is she afraid of me?*

"I was only told their given names," she informed him. "You must know I mistook the man called Jason for a new employee of my father's, or I would not be in this situation."

"Ramsey would have tried another strategy if you had not come with Jason. He had alternate plans. He was determined to bring you here," Steven volunteered.

"But why me?" Annie asked as if she were in deep thought trying to comprehend what she was hearing. What other plans did Ramsey have? Would he have taken her by force? Suppose she had not followed, thinking Jason was Kip Thornton? Was Jason, who gave the impression he was shy, and even showing signs of compassion, capable of harming her?

"Surely you know why," Steven said and looked at her questioningly. She looked like a piece of fine porcelain. She was every bit as beautiful as Jason said she was. There was something about this girl that he could not explain. She was so honest and sincere. He had never met anyone with such grace. She would be in a class of her own. His thoughts strayed to Darlene. Had she met her?

"No, I can't think of anything except the reason Louis gave me. He said it had to do with the pregnancy care center and adoption home. But why me? I am not connected to either of these except through my father. My father is helping to build these homes for the girls. What does Dr. Ramsey think taking me hostage will bring about there?" Annie asked this time and looked directly into Steven's startling blue eyes, waiting for an explanation.

"I better let Ramsey tell you in his time what his plan is concerning this whole matter. I am not directly involved in the clinic," Steven evaded the issue.

Annie ate a few bites of her breakfast without much interest.

How long would she be held here? Steven had said he was not directly connected with the clinic. Obviously he meant Dr. Ramsey's clinic, the Women's Clinic. He would not want to help Dr. Ramsey if he did not believe that abortion was all right. What did he do if he did not work for Ramsey? These thoughts clouded her mind. Why was she concerned with Steven Billups and his connection, anyway? She would never see him again when she was free. Or would she, would she even want to?

Steven sat on the sofa watching Annie intently until her eyes turned to his, and he turned his head to look across the room out the window. When would Ramsey decide to make his move, or was there a move to make? What was he really planning? Would he demand the antiabortion group to stop the construction of building the center as a type of ransom for his hostage? He looked back at Annie, sitting now with her head bowed. Was she praying? He spoke to her.

"What do you do to keep your thoughts occupied?" he questioned, breaking into her thoughts. After a moment or two she lifted her head, and he thought he saw a trace of tears in her eyes. She looked into his eyes briefly, then lowered her head to answer.

"There seems nothing to do except wait until Dr. Ramsey is finished with this foolishness," she answered resignedly.

"Would you like some magazines or books to read? I am sure there are some in the library downstairs. I can't believe he did not think of that, but perhaps he did, and Louis did not follow his orders," Steven offered.

"Perhaps, yes, I would like that," she said with humility. It seemed so easy to remain calm with Steven. He was so different from Louis. They were not in the same class, she thought. There was not a threat with Steven. But what did Louis say? He "charmed" the women? Was he charming her and then would change? She knew whatever, she must keep her head.

"Do you think you could get me a Bible?" she asked, looking at Steven. He was so good-looking sitting there so calm and confident. His dark hair curled just enough to hold itself in place. He had a neat, clean-cut look, broad shoulders, and lean hips and long legs that were strong. He was wearing dark trousers with expensive shoes. *Were they Rockports?* She had gone shopping with Christina and Nathan, and he wore Rockports. The mock turtleneck beneath his sweater was of the same shade of dark grey as his pants. The bold, gold watch on his wrist gleamed as his sleeve inched above it. Her eyes traveled to his hand. *There was no ring . . . did this mean that he was unmarried?*

At his age there was probably a fiancé. What did it matter to her? Why would she even think such a thought? This man was helping hold her captive, worrying her parents and keeping her from her life.

"A Bible?" he asked, with a cynical look on his face. Then he broke into a smile. "I doubt that Dr. Ramsey has a Bible in the house, but I can see no harm in trying to find out for you. I've never seen such a pretty girl carrying a Bible around. . . . I thought that was the practice of fat old ladies." He laughed at his own poor joke.

Annie looked at him and realized she had let his good looks take her mind off the fact that he was not one who loved God, as she did. His behavior had been such that she could have been fooled. *Was that part of his charm?*

"Mr. Billups, all ages and all sizes and shapes of people love God's Word. I happen to love reading from the Bible and do so every day. I left my New Testament in my car when I thought I was going to lunch with my father. Normally, I would have had it in my purse, but I was late on Friday leaving home and read a portion before going to class. Then I laid it on the seat and forgot to pick it up when Mr. . . . , I mean Jason, spoke to me beside the car," she explained, patiently and emphatically.

"Okay, that just happens to be my preconceived idea about the people who read that book. I read it myself as a child, but I found it quite boring mostly," he offered.

"Does that mean you will allow me to have one to read?" she asked again.

"I see no reason why you can't read while you are here. There are other things we could do together, but if you want I will go down and see what I can find. There is a television, but Ramsey felt it better that you not watch the news," he informed her.

"Why ever would he not want me to watch the news? He doesn't plan to harm my father in any way, does he?" Anxiety seeped into Annie's voice as she pondered such a thought.

"I am sure your father is safe. I am not sure about the TV, but perhaps I could check it out, and if he has changed his mind, we might could move one in. A DVD player would wile away hours with some choice movies," he said with a mischievous glint in his eye.

With this Steven went to the door and unlocked it. Turning in the doorway, he said, "You will not need to make your bed. The maid will be up to take care of that."

Annie heard the lock click, closing her in with her thoughts that were overwhelming her. It was almost midday on Saturday. What were her parents doing? Had her father gone to the police? Were her friends aware of her disappearance? What about Tony?

He was supposed to call her today. He was such a nice guy. She knew he cared for her more than she did him. He was a very good doctor, or so she had heard. There was a great future for him. He had wanted to see her more often than she cared to go out with him. What did Steven Billups do? Was he also a doctor? What was his connection with Dr. Ramsey? Arresting her thoughts, she smiled to herself. . . . Where did he come in her life? He was her guard!

How dare she even care what he did! Yet, was she not to care for all people and try to show them to Christ? Was she interested in his life because she was interested in him spiritually? Of course, what else?

She heard the key turn in the lock, and opening the door was a willowy, middle-aged lady with a basket of cleaning compounds and clean linens. She looked at Annie with eyes that told her that she did not approve of what was taking place here. She set her basket down and laid the linens on the arm of the sofa.

Sticking her hand out to Annie, she smiled and said, "I am Sally Brown, the maid and cook for the Manor."

Annie took Sally's hand in hers, a soft warm hand, the hand that could belong to a friend.

"I am Annie Marrow, pleased to meet you, Ms. Brown."

"Sally," the lady said with tenderness in her smile as she reached up and touched Annie's blonde curls. "I have never seen hair so beautiful before in my life," she said. "Just like an angel's and that smile, even in this situation."

"A pity," was her last words before she went into the bedroom to begin the work she was here to do.

The lock clicked, and "Sally, is that you?" a voice from the doorway boomed. An armful of magazines was placed on the table beside the sofa and turning with a big smile, Steven held out a big black Bible to Annie. He looked like a little boy who had been caught in the cookie jar, and Annie smiled sweetly as she took the Bible.

His hand caught hers in the exchange. It was a tender touch. Annie quickly pulled her hand away without being offensive.

She crossed the room to the chair directly in front of the window overlooking the back of the Manor where a stream cut though the landscape. Rain was falling in torrents, and the visibility was limited. Annie could make out the huge trees swaying in the wind as the rain washed them. Occasionally the wind blew the rain against the window making a loud swishing sound. It seemed the whole world was crying on the outside as Annie was crying on the inside. Being a person who liked her freedom, she felt depressed today.

One thing that she had to be thankful for, she kept trying to remind herself, was that Louis was not there. *Was Steven going to pose a problem?* She found herself having to be careful. Where she was repulsed by Louis, Steven was dangerous in another way . . . his charm . . . yes, that charm he used on all the women.

Sally finished her chores and picking up her basket and the dirty linens, she went to the door.

Shaking her head from side to side "A pity," was all that she could say before she inserted the key and locked the door behind her and was gone.

Annie opened the Bible and began to read aloud: "Let love be without dissimulation. Abhor that which is evil; cleave to that which is good. Be kindly affectioned one to another with brotherly love; in honor preferring one another. Not slothful in business; fervent in spirit; serving the Lord. Rejoicing in hope; patient in tribulation; continuing instant in prayer."

She stopped here. Annie sat for a long time looking out the window but not seeing. The room was dead quiet. Steven sat as though he was mesmerized. Her voice, when she read the Bible was so captivating. The look on her face was as though she was enjoying a great concert at Carnegie Hall. Her voice had been just that musical.

Wait a minute, Steven Billups. What is wrong with you? The charmer-of-all-women? Are you letting this little simple girl; yet, she wasn't a mere girl, she was a woman. . . . how old did Ramsey say she was? Oh yes, he said she was nineteen! Yet her wisdom surpassed many women he had known who were much older. He shook himself back into reality.

Breaking the spell, he said, "Now that you have had your Sunday School lesson on Saturday, could you and I do something more entertaining?"

Annie lowered her head a moment; then she threw it back, her blonde curls swinging softly about her shoulders. She looked him directly in the eye and asked, "And what would be entertaining to you, Mr. Billups?"

"Well, come over here by me on the sofa and let us get acquainted." He said then laughed a sensual laugh.

"Mr. Billups, you and I can get to know each other, and perhaps I already know something about you just by observation. I don't have to sit by you on the sofa to know you exercise a certain amount of charm on the opposite sex," Annie retaliated.

"Are you falling under my charm, Miss Marrow?" Steven asked teasingly.

"I find you more charming in your real self than the man of the world that you are masking," she said boldly. Was she right? Was this "charmer" a mask? Was this in order to be accepted? She knew many people put on a mask to be accepted in the world, thinking it would bring success, and even thinking it was necessary to get along in the world.

"I don't know what you mean," he countered. He was shocked to think this little ice maiden would dare accuse him of deceit.

"I see now what spurred Louis into action," he continued. "You are so young and naive that you don't realize you are encouraging the male ego to show you who is boss." He glared at her.

"I am sorry if I offended you with the truth of what I see," she came back. "You have the potential of being such a gentle, caring person. I found that to be true the first moment I opened my eyes and saw you."

"And what impression do you find now?" he questioned to taunt her.

"That you are afraid to really be what you were brought up to be," she did not back up in fear of him.

"What do you know about what I was brought up to be?" He was completely startled that she had hit on a truth, and it hurt his male ego to admit it to himself.

"I know nothing about you except those things I have observed, Mr. Billups," she answered boldly.

"Let's drop the subject," he insisted. "I'm bored. How can I stay here with you all day and night with nothing to do?" He was angry.

"You do not have to stay here with me, Mr. Billups. . . . "

He interrupted her . . . "Steven, Steven, is my name. And what is your name? Let me see, oh, yes, Annie, Annie the ice maiden."

"All right, Steven, you are free to go and entertain yourself somewhere else. I will not try to escape. Perhaps this is my tribulation that is to teach me patience. I realize I am captive here and until I am set free, I will try to find contentment," she said calmly and securely.

He stood beside the sofa as if to leave the suite, and as he did she spoke in her own sweet way.

"Thank you, Steven, for bringing me the Bible. You could not have done a nicer thing for me."

She looked down at her hands as she caught one in the other. He made no comment, just stood looking at her, unbelieving.

What kind of person was she? Had she never been attracted to the opposite sex in a physical way? Is that the reason her father could be so set on fighting the abortion issue? With this he walked to the door, unlocked it and left.

Annie sat down on the sofa and picked up a magazine, holding it as though she were reading it, yet she wasn't even aware of holding it at all. Her thoughts were muddled, and she could not seem to get them organized. What a predicament she was in! She compared the three men she had met since yesterday about this time — Jason, Louis, and now Steven. All different, and so much alike. Each frightening in his own way. She had not been exposed to many young men who were not Christians. That did make a difference.

Was God allowing her to see this side of life for a purpose? She had never really thought about what kind of situations brought young girls to yield their bodies to men they were only dating, or even sometimes had just met. This kind of action had always been so repulsive to her.

She had known from her early teens that she wanted to be pure before the Lord and have a clear conscience with all people concerning morality. She had been taught that a girl kept her mind clean and her body pure for one man. That man she would someday in the future come to love with all her heart. She expected the same from the man who would be her life partner. As yet, that Mr. Right had not come along.

What kind of person did Steven want to be? Was he attracted to the woman who had poor moral values? What had he been like as a little boy? This thought brought a smile to her face as she visualized him as a little boy. She almost laughed out loud. What was she doing thinking of him? She reprimanded herself.

Steven had left the suite angry. He did not know what he was angry about. He went into the kitchen as Sally was preparing lunch.

"A pity, a pity," she was muttering.

"Sally, what are you muttering about?" he asked as he poured his coffee and spooned in creamer.

"That poor child upstairs! Just a pity. She is so beautiful. A shame to close up such an angel and keep her away from this old ugly world. God just gave us a few gems to enjoy, and she is one of them," she muttered.

Steven fell silent. Sally was right about one thing; Annie Marrow was beautiful. In all her simplicity, without the aid of a lot of makeup, she was an eye-catcher. There was something else . . . her purity . . . what was it like? An untouched flower that had bloomed out fresh on a warm spring day? There was a fragrance about her that was captivating. He remembered her reading the Bible.

What had she read? "Abhor that which is evil" Could that be her secret? Had she been touched by the evil of this world? She had such a tender look about her. What had Sally said? "A pity." It would be a pity to see her harmed by anyone he knew, especially by himself. *Had he hurt her with his taunts?* She was strong as she stood up to him. A smile played on his lips as he remembered her bold remarks.

But what about Louis? He would not hesitate to step on such a delicate plant. Did he harm her last night? Was that the reason she was so afraid this morning when he bent over her? Had she slept poorly, afraid for her safety? She was a spitfire, all right!

But there was something about her that he could not seem to forget. He had never met anyone who had claimed his thoughts any more than this little Annie Marrow. . . . Sally was talking to him, and he had missed what she was saying. He caught the last few words.

"That Darlene, she could do her harm!"

"Is Darlene in the Manor, Sally?" he asked.

"Yes, Mr. Steven, and she and that no-good Louis are not to be trusted." Sally stalked to the pantry to get the pan she needed.

"You don't really believe Darlene would attack Annie . . . Miss Marrow," he caught himself. She had become Annie in his thoughts, but he must guard his thoughts. *What had she said about him? That he wore a mask at times. Did he?*

"I better go in and see if Dr. Ramsey is in his suite," Steven informed Sally. "If you need me before I return, ring his number." With this he crossed the foyer to the right wing of the Manor.

Annie had no idea how long she had let her thoughts run unleashed. She looked at her watch. It was almost one o'clock. She was not hungry, but she knew food would be arriving shortly.

Who would bring it? Steven was bored with her. He was used to more exciting company. There he was in her thoughts again. The clicking of the lock alerted Annie to someone entering the suite.

"Well, Miss Marrow, did you sleep well last night?" Darlene asked and grinned a sly grin. "Or did you want Louis to stay and entertain you?" She knew she was irritating Annie.

"I was extremely happy you came along, Darlene," Annie said thoughtfully. "He seems the type you would be attracted to."

"Are you saying he's not good enough for you?" Darlene taunted. "Louis has quite a different story than the one you are trying to make me believe. You better leave him alone! I came here to warn you about trying to charm Louis. He is mine! Do you understand?" Darlene was wild with jealousy, and Louis played on this fact.

Annie stared at Darlene. What had Louis told her to get her into such a rage? Should she defend herself or let it go? Annie stood with a magazine in her hand trying to decide what was her best defense.

Darlene, in her rage, caught the long blonde hair and pulling Annie to the sofa began to strike her across the face.

Annie let out a cry, trying to free herself. She managed to stand just as Darlene slapped her. Annie fell. She did not remember anything else clearly, but when she was able to focus her eyes, she saw Steven pushing Darlene out into the corridor.

She saw his face, fuzzily, close to hers. He had his arms around her drawing her close to his strong body. She was too weak to resist. Her head fell on his shoulder, and he brushed the hair back from her face as he rubbed his hand over the dark red spot on her cheek. Annie was powerless. She could not muster up enough strength to disentangle herself from his arms.

Tears flowed in torrents from her eyes like the rain had done earlier that day. These were tears she had held back since she had realized she had been taken hostage. Steven took a clean fresh handkerchief from his pocket and wiped her eyes.

She barely heard him whisper, "Everything is going to be all right, Annie." He seemed to be in no hurry to let her go, and she needed someone to just be near.

Steven could smell the subtle fragrance of the blonde curls that lay close to his face as he looked over her head unseeing.

She was such a delicate person, no match physically for raging Darlene. He liked the idea of comforting her. This had never been his role before. She seemed so unafraid of him at the moment. Was it because she needed a friend, someone she did not feel threatened with? He could taste the saltiness of the blood from the cut beside his lip that Darlene had given him as he separated her from Annie. That cut from Darlene's fingernail would have been Annie's as Darlene reached to bring the nail down the cheek she had slapped. Darlene must be kept out of this suite!

Suddenly realizing where she was, Annie began to struggle in his arms. He released her.

She looked at him and smiled, a shy embarrassed smile, and spoke, "I am sorry to have been in need of a strong shoulder. You certainly know how to console a frightened female. Thank you for rescuing me.

"Fighting has never been one of my strong points. I have no experience in that area. Not having brothers or sisters, I was spared that experience, I suppose. In our home a good strong argument was all that was allowed, and after that you were sent to your room to form a definite opinion. If you discovered you were in the wrong, apologies were in order," she seemed to be rattling on to cover up the embarrassment of finding herself in his arms.

CHAPTER TEN

The windshield wipers moved back and forth to a rhythm as the car sped through the traffic. Bob Thomason and Andrew spoke occasionally. They seemed to be in deep thought as they traveled to the Watertown Police Station. It had been twenty-four hours since Annie was due home, and no word had been heard from her.

"Andrew," Pastor Thomason spoke hesitantly, "I called Gregory last night and asked him to do a little investigating as I knew Annie was a reliable person. I explained that she was dependable. He put a detective on the case. I trust he will have something today that will help us to understand what is going on."

"You are a true friend and have been a real source of strength to us through this ordeal." Andrew said. "Julia and I have always appreciated you and Lori, but this has drawn us together more than anything. You know, I believe that is why trials come sometimes to give us opportunity to see how much we need the fellowship of the church. My prayer is that they have found some lead in the case."

They were turning into the parking lot and parking the car in the first available space. They locked the car and started toward the large white building. Andrew had passed this building many times and thought how grateful he was that he had never had to come down to the station to get Annie out of trouble. Now here he was. She was definitely in trouble, but not of her own making. Of that he was sure.

"We have an appointment with Chief Garrison," Andrew announced to the sergeant at the desk.

The sergeant looked up from his writing and asked, "Your name, please?" and recognizing Andrew he said, "Oh, you are Andrew Marrow, are you not? I just want to shake your hand, Mr. Marrow. I believe in the project you have been working on. It takes courage to take a stand in something so controversial. I will tell the chief you are here."

He disappeared into a hallway, and coming back to the desk he said, "You can go in now. He will be off the phone by the time you reach his office."

"Thank you," Andrew said and shook hands with the man again along with Pastor Thomason and walked down the hallway.

Tapping lightly on the door, Andrew heard a voice respond with a hearty "Come in!"

The big man behind the desk stood up, and, reaching across the desk, he shook first Andrew's hand and then Pastor Thomason's. He was a strong-looking man with dark hair that was sprinkled with gray at the temples. His eyes were brown, and heavy brows that almost came together across his nose gave him a slightly sinister look. His broad shoulders bulged as he moved his chair up so that he could rest his chin on his hands, leaning forward with great intenseness as he listened to Andrew.

"Annie has never before failed to arrive home at an appointed time. There was a time she did not come home when we thought she should, but she called to say her car failed to start and she would be late. That is why we were certain something out of the ordinary had happened to her." Andrew said and looked directly into the eyes of Gregory Garrison.

"Andrew, we started an investigation last evening after a call from Bob here. And sad to say, as yet there is nothing substantial to go on. We do have a few speculations that I need to discuss with you." Chief Garrison opened his desk and brought forth papers and a pen.

"There are questions we need to ask, and from time to time there will be others," he said. "I am sure you understand there was very little to go on. Was Annie involved in any way in the pregnancy center project that you are so much a part of?" the chief asked, pencil poised.

"No, in no way directly. She is wholly supportive of our plans and aware of the opposition. She has helped in the present office a few times with the filing. As far as being involved in the actual plans for the new endeavors, I would have to say she was not," Andrew answered with much feeling.

"I understand there have been some threats to various members of the board working on the center and that construction is starting today. Have you received any threats?" Garrison asked, leaning back and watching Andrew with much interest.

"No, we have not received any threats of any kind. We have an unlisted number. Perhaps, that has saved us. We felt when Annie was entering her teen years that an unlisted number would be better, and we have kept it since I have taken this project to heart." Andrew answered and looked at his hands as he rubbed the palms together.

"I know that you have not endorsed any protest against the Women's Clinic here," Chief Garrison continued. "I realize you have gone to more constructive ideas as providing an alternative which would give a real solution while waiting for legislation to go through to prevent many of the problems of our young people. I could not find any evidence that showed you had personally confronted any of the doctors who are performing abortions. I have heard a few of your speeches to civic organizations and felt that the way you have handled your stand against this dilemma is a very sensible one."

Chief Garrison looked at Andrew with admiration.

"Do you think Annie's disappearance has something to do with my involvement in the fight against abortion, Gregory?" Andrew asked directly.

"At this point, we have to look into every area of involvement of your entire family." Chief Garrison tapped his pencil on his desk and sat back in his swivel chair, deep in thought.

There was silence for a moment as the three men, each in his own conscience began a mind-searching process.

"This is your daughter's first year at Jefferson Community College, I am told. Has she made any new friends that she has told you about?" The chief was exploring every area that he could think of.

"She has made some new acquaintances, and she has mentioned a few, but there has been no conflict with them. Annie was always rather easy to get along with as a child, and she is a young woman of compassion and care," Andrew said.

"We are keeping our eyes open and running checks on a few areas at present, but there is so little we know now that I feel we need to give time for the on-going investigation. I realize time is agonizing for you and Mrs. Marrow. I hate that it has to be this way, but I do hope you understand," Chief Garrison said.

"Yes, Gregory, we do. We appreciate your efforts. If I told you we were not worried, I would be lying, but we know that Annie is not lost in the eyes of our great God. We have committed her to His care. Do not hesitate to call us at any hour if you should have any questions or if we could aid the process of investigation," Andrew said with a note of sadness.

Bob Thomason had sat quietly during the entire questioning and thought about the many times he had been in the presence of Chief Garrison with other parents not in the same situation.

Often times Garrison had tried to help them with children who had been arrested. As he listened to Andrew speak of his faith, Bob realized the man had lived his faith in good times, and now it was his strength in this time of distress.

The chief rose from his chair, and reaching across his desk again, he clasped Andrew's hand in his big one.

With compassion and concern he whispered, "You are right about that." Turning to Bob Thomason he shook his hand and said, "You men keep praying for us."

After the men left the police station and were on their way home, Bob said, "I thank God for the testimony of your family. Even in this, your faith is there to show the world. I believe God will see you through in a victorious way."

CHAPTER ELEVEN

After the episode with Darlene and finding herself in Steven's arms, Annie was a little shaken. She somehow could not forget how comfortably she had allowed him to console her. She had cried on his shoulder, and the touch of his hand on her cheek was so tender.

Just the memory of the soft caressing way he ran his strong tanned hand over the reddened spot . . . in her fright and shock she was too numb to realize just what was happening, yet now she could remember how gentle his touch was and how he held her to his body in a way that calmed her every fear. *How long had he been holding her before she came to full realization of the situation?*

She remembered him brushing her hair back, and seeing the mark of Darlene's hand, he had uttered a word. *What was it?* She could not remember. That was when all gates broke loose and her flood of tears flowed like a waterfall. He had called her "Annie" for the first time.

Annie felt so ashamed to be brought back to consciousness and knowledge that she had fallen so freely into his arms for consoling. It was after this that she saw his lip where Darlene's fingernail had dug into the flesh and left its mark, a wound that would have been hers had not Steven interfered. Annie was still struggling with the emotion she felt then. It was something she had never felt before -- compassion mixed with gratitude but something more, something unidentifiable. Steven had waited until he was assured that she was all right before he left the suite. Annie had gone into the bathroom for a wet cloth to clean the wound, but Steven took it from her as if he was afraid of her touch. She felt a small sense of rejection at his action. He held the cloth on his lip and left the suite.

Annie was looking at herself in the mirror above the bathroom sink. Her hair was disheveled and the red mark was still visible. She ran cold water over a fresh cloth and held it on the bruise. Perhaps a shower would make her feel better, she reasoned.

Would Steven return before she could get finished? She locked the bedroom door and prepared for her bath. . . .

Drying herself off, Annie kept thinking how much better she felt. She looked at her skirt and sweater. They looked so much in need of cleaning and pressing.

Did she dare wear one of the outfits that been provided for her by the eminent Dr. Ramsey? Opening the sliding closet door, she reached in to touch the garments hanging so orderly in there. She selected a sky blue wool flannel dress. The softness of the material told her that it was an expensive dress. Pulling it over her blonde curls that were bouncing from the dampness of the shower, she looked into the mirror. The blue of the fabric accented the blue of her eyes.

She buttoned the three buttons of the bodice and smoothed the skirt into place. Amazing, how well it fit. *How had Ramsey known her size? Was it a coincidence? How could it be?* Annie ran the comb through her hair until it shone with golden lights; then she worked the makeup into her delicate skin to hide the mark of battle. She rummaged through her purse to find the soft peach lipstick, and a smile played on her lips. At least she would look her best if she had to live in such close quarters.

There were shoes in the closet that went well with the dress. She chose the navy flats and completed her outfit. She thought again how much better off she was than Paul had been when he was in prison. He had been in a dungeon, and she shuddered to think of the darkness and dampness of such an idea.

What had Paul written from that place? "For I have learned, in whatsoever state I am, therewith to be content." Annie remembered reading that verse from Philippians, but she could not remember what verse or chapter it was in. Annie almost felt guilty that she felt such contentment. *Was this trust?*

Satan would not want her to be content. He was the one who wanted her to fret when she could not help herself. God wanted her to trust Him and let Him deliver her.

Annie unlocked the bedroom and returned to the sitting room. She pulled the chair close to the window looking out over the back lawn. The rain had subsided, and the darkness was enveloping the earth. It was still early, and she knew dinner would not be up for some time.

She had not eaten much at lunch after Darlene's visit. She found herself looking forward to Sally's food. She picked up the big black Bible and turned to Philippians to find the verse she had been given.

. . .

Steven had gone to the adjoining room where the three guys were to alternate staying as they were on shifts. He had not spent much time there since he had come on duty that morning early. His mind went back to that time. He thought about the feelings that had flooded over him during those few hours. He had been so confident about this little job before he walked into that bedroom this morning. . . . *Was it just this morning? Only about six hours ago?*

He went to the mirror and cleaned the wound on his lip. After washing the blood from the wound he realized it would soon heal, and no great damage had been done. *But what could that red fingernail have done to Annie's frail delicate face?* He was only glad he had come back up to bring her lunch when he did.

78

Darlene was in one of her rages, and Annie was taken so unaware. He was shocked at the sight of Annie on the floor as a result of Darlene's blow. Without really thinking about what Annie would think, he had come between them and, pushing Darlene out the door, had lifted Annie in his arms. She appeared to be in shock. Her blue eyes were closed and she clung to him, he was sure, unaware of what she was doing.

He had felt so comfortable holding her, consoling her; it was all so innocent. When the tears started, he wanted to kiss them away, but restrained himself. How glad he was that he had at this time. *What would Annie have thought? She did not know what he was really like. What had she said about him that had bothered him so? That he wore a mask to be accepted in this world? Was she right? He had had that mask in place so long it had become a part of him.*

As he ran a comb through his dark hair he was reminded of the fragrance of blonde curls close to his face. She smelled so clean. She was clean and pure, he was convinced of that. Would he get bored with a girl like her? Would dating someone like her get monotonous? He was accustomed to girls who enjoyed his "charming."

If he were wearing a mask, it was there to attract girls of a certain type. He had never met anyone quite like Annie.

Steven showered and changed into a cream-striped shirt and dark trousers that matched the navy stripe in his shirt. His clean-shaven face had only a trace of the sign from the scrimmage of the afternoon. He splashed aftershave on and left the room.

"Sally, what's for dinner?" Steven asked, sniffing under lids.

"Mr. Steven, you know I don't like you looking into my pots and pans. I am making something special for our little angel upstairs. She eats like a bird. I know it's because of grief over this awful situation. I am making pot roast. I believe she would like that and strawberry shortcake for dessert," Sally said and beamed.

"Mr. Steven, you ought not to have gotten mixed up in this thing.

That little angel is so sweet," she continued as she stirred her cake.

"I know, Sally. Perhaps you are right, but I am and there's no getting out at this point in time. Anyway, do I want out right now? What do you think about me having my dinner in the suite with Miss Marrow? Do you think she would object too much?" he asked Sally, looking for her expression as a sign.

"Mr. Steven, since it's you, I think the little angel might welcome your company. She has been cooped up in that suite now for over twenty-four hours, and she looks like a free bird to me. Why don't I set up a small game table and make it real special for her? It might take some of the sadness out of those big eyes. Don't she have the prettiest blue eyes you ever saw -- So clear and pure?" Sally asked without looking at Steven.

"Yes," was all Steven said as he was in deep thought, unwilling to even become conscious of what those thoughts were.

Annie was reading the accounts from Philippians. Paul had been such a witness of God's grace in this prison. That is what I want to be also, she thought.

She leaned her head against the windowsill and began praying, unaware that the door had been opened.

"Dear God, I am afraid I have failed You so often in witnessing. I do want to show Your grace in my life. Thank you, Father, for Sally. I felt a oneness with her. You have given me a friend in my distress. Lord, I pray for Louis. You know what change needs to take place in his life. He needs to see Jesus as I know Him. And Darlene, help me to be patient with her and let her see the witness of Your love in my life. She needs to be loved by someone who loves her for the right reasons. Jason needs you, Father."

She paused in her prayer, the person at the door wondering if he were found out in his appearance there. He wanted to leave, but somehow he could not bring himself to do so. Was she going to say anything to God about him? Should he listen? This was between her and God.

"And Steven, Father . . . " a break was in her voice . . . "he has such potential for being such a dear man. He was so kind to me today. Father, touch his heart in a special way. Remove that mask and let the real person show. You know all our needs, but You said to bring our hearts desires to You and You would fulfill them. These are mine. Please bless my parents, comfort them and somehow reveal to them that I am safe. Thank you in Jesus' precious name. Amen." The prayer ended and she sat still and silent.

The door was eased silently closed; she never knew of anyone else's presence.

Steven waited quietly in the hall for a long time. He kept hearing her voice in such sincerity. *Was she real? A lot of people were fakes and pretended to be religious. Could she be one of them?* Finally he opened the door and stepped into the suite.

With a big smile, he looked around the back of the wing chair and asked, "You all right?"

"Yes, and you?" She looked at him. A brightness shone in her eyes at the sight of his appearance in his clean, neat clothes. Every hair was in place, and he looked more handsome than ever -- part of his charm, no doubt.

Steven caught his breath at the sight of her. He had to guard his feelings. *Was she aware of the effect she was having on him?*

"You look like someone who needs to have a special surprise for dinner," he said for lack of anything to say. Her loveliness made him stammer.

"Well, it became a necessity that I wear some of the clothes that were provided. I guess I should be grateful that Dr. Ramsey had studied me so completely that he knew my exact size. How he ever knew, I don't know, although I am a popular size, I suppose."

"He could not have chosen anything that matched your eyes any better," Steven said looking into her eyes, hating to have to look away.

"Thank you, I take that kind word as you are paying me as well as

Dr. Ramsey a compliment," she said with a smile as though she was pleased with his admiration of her.

"Sally is preparing a special dinner for you. Would you mind if I shared it with you here in the suite?" he asked, holding his breath for an answer. How out of character for him to almost plead for an opportunity to spend time over dinner with a girl. He had never had to do that. There had always been girls in his life, and they were eager for his attention.

Annie thought for a moment, hesitating before she answered. It would be rather nice to have someone to share her meal. She had always hated eating alone. She had almost always had her meals with her parents or her friends. She looked at Steven with a little grin. He thought the grin was prompted by some mischievous thought.

"Mr. Billups, I accept your invitation to dinner. Are you sure our reservations are secured?" Annie was making a game of dinner.

Steven, bowing, answered, "Quite sure, Miss Marrow. Shall we dine at seven?" He went along with her game.

Annie laughed for the first time since she had been brought here. Steven thought what a lovely sound her laugh was. To think she could laugh and joke in spite of the fact of her being held against her will. Most girls would be so angry they would break everything in this room.

CHAPTER TWELVE

The evening passed quickly as the Marrows and Thomasons talked of the visit with Chief Garrison. They discussed the question of Annie's disappearance and the possible connection with the pregnancy center and placement home. What was expected to be accomplished, if this was the reason? After a time the Thomasons reluctantly left, hating to leave Julia and Andrew alone. It was imperative that they go, as Pastor Thomason needed to look over his sermon for the next day.

Julia and Andrew had turned the television on but were interrupted by the doorbell. Andrew opened the door to find Christina, Nathan and Tony bearing a big basket of fruit.

"We wanted to come by and keep you company," Nathan said, trying to be cheerful. "You don't mind, do you?"

"Of course, we don't mind, you kids are a great comfort to us. Come on in," Andrew answered in all sincerity.

"Julia, the kids are here," he called out.

"I guess Andrew will think of you as kids until you have kids of your own," Julia said, linking her arm in Andrew's. "Please come into the den. What a pretty and delicious looking fruit basket!" Taking the basket she set it on the table behind the couch.

"We had a hard time thinking of something to bring, and we all saw this basket and decided that it looked too pretty to pass up," Christina said, hugging Julia.

"Has there been any word of Annie?" Tony asked with concern. "I know you are tired of being asked that question."

"Not at all, Tony, we know you, her friends, are as concerned as we are. And the answer is no. No word at all. They say no news is good news, and we must believe she is all right." Andrew answered with his hand on Tony's broad shoulder.

"What did Chief Garrison think about the situation? Or can we discuss that?" Nathan asked as he leaned forward in the big wingback chair that was beside the fireplace.

"Of course, we must keep this as quiet as possible so the media will not get wind of it, but you are entitled to know any news we have. Garrison had done some investigating on the recommendation of Pastor Thomason before we went yesterday.

"Nothing concrete has been found. He is leaning toward the involvement that I have with the pregnancy care center and placement home. He is inclined to think since the other members have had some mild threats made to them that it is possible someone has gone farther and taken Annie to somehow prevent the construction of the buildings. It sounds so farfetched to me. What could they possibly accomplish with such a plan? I realize that when people are stirred up and angry, they make unreasonable decisions convincing themselves that they are making good decisions." Andrew shook his head.

"I trust if this is the case that Annie is not forced against her will to be involved in anything that would have lasting effects on all our lives and especially hers." Andrew bowed his head, unable to face what he was really thinking.

"Does he think it is the people who are patients or the general public who believe that abortion is the alternative?" Tony asked and looked at Andrew with deep interest.

"I'm not sure. This thought is so premature, I think it was just a nucleus thought on his part," Andrew answered.

"I realize that should the home for women who are caught in a crisis of pregnancy without any kind of help from the other partner or even without support from their family be built, and the women see the real truth of abortion, that it could cause reason for concern for clinics or physicians who are using this means to make money. Are you aware of anyone in Watertown who majors on this type of procedure?" Tony speculated.

"Well, Tony, we are all aware that the Women's Clinic performs abortions, but whether they are in it in a wholesale way or not, we are just speculating. The board I have been involved with has known that some cases were sent out of town. Perhaps this was a safety measure to hide the real truth from the community. Our group does not stage protests; therefore, we do not come in direct confrontation with anyone in particular that is pushing abortion on a large scale. We have had parents to contact us who have learned their daughters had, without the parents' consent, gone to the clinic and secured an abortion. But how extensive the number of abortions here goes, we are not perfectly sure. I know you cannot reveal any knowledge you may have from exposure at the Good Samaritan, and I would not want to jeopardize your career to do so. What is your real opinion on abortion as a young physician and Christian?" Andrew finally asked.

"Mr. Marrow, I will not hesitate to tell you that until I became a Christian two years ago and was shown the truth from God's Word, I had not given it much thought other than the surgical procedure that I had observed. And of course, with the knowledge that has come to light concerning the actual growth of the fetus by those closely associated with gynecology, I am more convinced that life begins at conception. Since I am in the general practitioner field, I am limited in certain areas of surgery. I know now the harm in many instances that comes from the patient having an abortion. I have seen first hand a case of deep depression, and I attribute the problem to the patient's having an abortion before she was married. There are other cases under study at the time to document the danger of the procedure. If for no other reason, the fact that a mother has not given that little person an opportunity to life and to become all that God has desired him or her to be, is reason enough to convince me," Tony said.

"I wish others would look at it from the humanitarian view, if for no other reason," Andrew said. "But of course you cannot expect someone who does not know God and does not therefore care about pleasing God to take the Biblical view. That is the reason we came upon the idea of providing the home for a shelter during the crisis and seeing that the women had the best of care, in instances where they had no one. Then if each could find a job and housing and become self-supporting and desired to keep her baby, we would help in any way possible; if not, and the mother decided to adopt, our adoption placement team would work through the legal process to find a Christian home for the child.

"We believe this is an alternative to abortion. Just telling someone she should keep the baby and not providing a way puts that person in a place of desperation even more. There is a place for all kind of work in this fight against the loss of potential lives," Andrew said convincingly.

"Have the police questioned any of the students at the school?" Nathan asked.

"As far as I know, they have inquired about Annie and shown her picture to see if anyone remembers seeing her on Friday," Andrew answered.

The women had gone to the kitchen to make coffee and at this time returned with trays of cake and coffee. They set the tray on the table behind the sofa, and the men gathered around to help themselves.

CHAPTER THIRTEEN

Sally came through the suite door with a game table in one hand and a tablecloth in the other. She was a small woman but accustomed to heavy work. She had been at the Manor for years, serving the owner since she was a mere teenager. She knew the things that pleased almost anyone.

"Here, Sally," Steven said, jumping to his feet. "Let me have that table."

He took the table from her and began to open the legs out, at the same time looking about the room to find an ideal spot to put it. He decided to move a chair and put the table to the left of the fireplace placing it near the wall, so that it was in an out-of-the-way place and looked rather cozy. Sally immediately spread the creamy Battenberg cloth on, carefully seeing that each side was hanging perfectly. She returned to the corridor and from a large basket that she had brought up earlier, she began to arrange the china and silverware properly. In the center of the table, to match the ivory colored plates trimmed with pink apple blossoms, she placed a silver candleholder with double pink tapers and around it arranged dark violet chrysanthemums that she had found on the grounds in the flower beds that Annie had seen when she was brought to the Manor.

Sally walked over to Annie, standing observing all the ceremony of preparation for dinner.

"Are you all right, Angel?" she asked, touching Annie's cheek. "If Sally can, she will make this time as easy as is in her power," she said with determination in her voice.

Annie smiled at Sally, and her eyes filled with a strange light.

"Thank you, Sally, you are a true friend of mine, and I sense you are a friend of God."

"Oh, yes, Miss Marrow, God has seen me through many trials, and I knew when I first saw you that you were one of His. You can just tell. You know, it's like the Spirit tells you." Sally turned to leave. "Miss Marrow, God will deliver. You just keep that in mind." And with that she was gone.

Steven had watched this display of love from Sally to Annie and love returned. How had Sally known?

The meal was brought up by Sally and the young girl, Rosena, who Sally told Annie was her granddaughter. Rosena, Annie learned, helped in times when Sally could not handle everything.

"Mr. Steven, I'm leaving the serving to you for our little angel. I have other guests in the dining room to serve shortly. You know what to do," Sally said manner-of-factly and left the suite.

Steven and Annie laughed at Sally and her in-charge manner. She was a love, and Steven admired her as much as Annie did.

Steven spoke first, "Miss Marrow, follow me; I will lead you to your table." He stepped before Annie and pulled out the chair beside the table.

Annie graciously sat down, smiled up into his eyes and said, "Thank you, Mr. Billups." His eyes were the bluest she had ever seen, and there was a tenderness there before a shutter came down.

Steven took the chair opposite her, and they sat for an instant smiling at each other. Annie was the first to speak.

"Do you mind if I silently give thanks?" she requested sweetly, not assuming that he would want to participate in the giving of thanks.

Steven could only shake his head in acknowledgement that he did not mind. She bowed her head for a brief moment then lifted her eyes to his smiling ones as though nothing else in the world mattered except this moment.

Steven reached for her crystal wine glass, and from a bottle he poured a sparkling drink of burgundy color. After filling his own glass, keeping his eyes on her face to catch her expression, he said, "I knew you would not drink wine, so I purchased this sparkling grape juice instead."

On his face was a sly grin as he lifted his glass in a toast and said, "To Sally and her ideas."

Annie lifted her glass and sipped the bright liquid, not understanding exactly what Steven had meant. But she knew what she felt for Sally, and a toast for her was in order.

Steven served the dinner expertly. He was so handsome in the candlelight. His olive complexion took on a darker color causing his eyes to be darker and bluer. He seemed to be enjoying the meal equally as much as Annie. Ironic, she thought, she was actually enjoying this as though it was a regular date with one of her friends. On second thought, she had not remembered a time she had enjoyed anyone's presence as much as she had his . . . a danger signal went off in her brain . . . "a charmer"! Was that what Steven was doing? Was he charming her as a cat charms his prey and pounces?

"Where are you and who are you with, Miss Marrow?" Steven was asking as he sat calmly drinking his coffee after the meal.

"I'm sorry," Annie apologized for her inattentiveness. "I really was in a dream world, wasn't I?" She was thinking how glad she was he could not know what she was dreaming about.

"And what do you dream about?" He leaned forward as if to catch every word.

"Oh, my dreams are no different than any other woman's. All women enjoy being catered to, treated special and made to feel important. I was thinking that was just how I was feeling, in this situation. Thank you for making dinner special, Steven." She said his name with much feeling, or so it seemed to Steven.

"Tell me about yourself, Annie. What do you do? What are your hobbies, likes and dislikes?" Steven leaned on his elbow and looked across the flickering candles. How the soft light played on her beautiful features. Her nose was just the right length and turned up just slightly on the end to give her a look of dignity. The lashes that cast shadows on her soft cheeks. . . . Steven could feel the softness of the fair cheeks, remembering brushing his hand across her cheek where Darlene had struck her. The golden lights emanated from her hair as the flickering candle cast its light . . . her lips, with just a touch of pink gloss, that had been so inviting when he had held her . . . oh, how glad he was that he had held himself in check . . . yet even now he wanted to feel those lips on his. Shaking himself back to reality, he waited for her answer.

"I am an only child of two loving parents. I came to know Jesus as my personal Savior at an early age, and as you know, I'm what most people call a fanatic about reading the Bible." With this she chuckled and in a teasing way she went on, "I attend or was attending Jefferson Community College. If I fail to leave here soon, I could be dropped from class. I have a hobby of writing. I love writing short stories about real live instances. I like people and working with them. My dislikes are spinach and violence." She laughed and asked, "Does that pretty well sum up what you are wanting to know?"

Steven wanted to know much more than that about this unusual woman. But in this time and place he could never achieve his goal.

"Do I have the same right as a hostage here, to ask you the same question?" She was looking at him with a mischievous grin on her face.

"Let's forget about that part of it and remember we are having

90

dinner at a famous restaurant." He replied, hating this situation that she was in. "I'm afraid my life is going to be boring and maybe repulsive to you, Annie," he said with a slight hesitancy. Should he answer her questions?

"I think you are playing unfairly, Steven," she came back at him. "Let me be the judge of how I feel about you." She thought that came across rather awkwardly. Did she want to know how she felt about this strange man?

"I am one of three children of loving parents. I happen to be the only boy. I have two sisters who are older than me. The spoiled youngest child and a boy at that." He joked, fearing to go much further.

"I always wanted to make things well -- animals, people -- and even played with great imagination that I was the doctor and my stuffed animals were the patients. So . . . I am a doctor at Good Samaritan . . . a pediatrician. Can you imagine? I am around crying, sick babies constantly. I feel very comfortable in this profession and hope to set up practice in Watertown. I am from a small town outside of Chicago. I have hobbies but have had to forego them during these past several years as my schooling claimed all my time . . . well, almost all my time." He thought about the women that had been in his life. They were so different from the one who was looking so intently at him at the moment.

"I like to play tennis, and almost any sport. I, too, dislike violence and spinach, in that order," he laughed. He felt he had gotten out of that admirably.

"What about your spiritual life, Steven?" she had to ask, hoping that what she feared was not what she would hear.

"Oh, I believe in God. I was brought up to go to church. I never much liked it, but I know there is a God," he answered proudly.

Annie decided to overlook the obvious, that Steven, like so many people she had met, believed there was a God but believed that God was not personally involved in his life. He knew nothing of personally depending on Him.

"Steven, may I ask you another question?" Without waiting for an answer she asked, "Why are you mixed up in this scheme?"

"Well, I don't have to answer that, you know." He sounded resentful that she had brought it up, but Annie had to know why, one way or another.

"No, I suppose not, but it puzzles me. You are different from Louis and Darlene, and even Jason, and I see no resemblance to Dr. Ramsey except that you and he share the same profession," she replied, looking directly at him.

"In this life, you have to do some things to get ahead. Recommendations are very important in my profession. One physician can help another or he can hinder him. Dr. Ramsey is a powerful man in the medical profession. Every young and upcoming doctor looks to him as one in control. They are flattered when he recognizes them, and if they can get in his good graces, so to speak, they feel their success is almost inevitable. I need his confidence and help. When he approached me about this job, it sounded so simple. To guard a girl for twenty-four hours on my days away from the hospital for a substantial amount of money and the approval and, perhaps, recommendation from the eminent Dr. Ramsey. What is so bad about that? Have I been such a bad companion, Annie?" He was using all the charm he could muster to influence her answer.

"Do you really think you need his influence to make a success? Would your efforts not merit success? You obviously have studied hard, have compassion for the patients and the ability to put the things you have learned into practice. What else would you need? Could you not through the years be recognized, by the patients whom your life touches, as a capable doctor? In turn, those patients would remember and want to trust their children to your care," she tried to reason.

"You make it sound so simple, little Annie. You really know nothing about what it takes to break into this profession. It is not as simple as your life has seemingly been. What do you really know about life and the complications of it?" He was angry, and did not really know why. Who was she to judge his actions? Just a young woman who had experienced so little of life, untouched by even feelings for a man. Was that what bothered him about the whole situation? Was she so naive or was she stupid?

"Steven, when do you think Dr. Ramsey will release me?" she asked sincerely, changing the subject.

"I can't say. I am totally unaware of his plans, as I told you. I was hired to be your guard . . . companion for as long as he needed me. He gave me no idea of the time when he first spoke with me. I know he means no harm to you or I would not have agreed to take the job. You know I told you I hate violence," Steven reminded her. His anger had subsided slightly.

"Do you agree, as a doctor, with Dr. Ramsey's practice of abortion?" she questioned even though she feared a confrontation.

"Why not?" he answered with defiance in his voice. "I think a woman should be able to choose what she wants to do with her own body!" he answered emphatically not really thinking through his answer.

"Do you think the idea of stopping abortion takes away the right from the woman to choose for herself?" she asked simply.

"Well, doesn't it? If she could not choose, she would be having the responsibility for a child she did not want!" he said harshly as if to intimate that she was stupid not to see the point.

"Well, I choose to disagree with you. I feel she has already made a choice in the matter," Annie answered firmly, looking at him with her chin tilted and causing that little turned up nose to have even more dignity.

"You believe she can control her body not to conceive?" he asked with a leering look as though he was talking to a simpleton.

"Yes," she said. "She can choose to limit her sexual activity to the confines of marriage. That is not impossible, you know, even though this world paints the picture that sex is the way of expressing love and must be expressed regardless of the situation," she said throwing her napkin down and getting to her feet. She walked to the window.

"Is that what you have chosen, Annie?" he said as he stood closely behind her.

"Yes, I feel it is important that I keep myself pure for the man I someday will fall in love with. I expect the man to do the same. Love is expressed in many ways, and the intimacy of the sex act is reserved for marriage as an ultimate expression.

"It's like this . . . there are many things as a little girl that I was looking forward to when I became a certain age. Losing a tooth and the tooth fairy coming when that time arrived, going to school when I became old enough. At three, I wanted to go to school and was told I must wait until I was five. I did not want to wait, but five was a very exciting age because of the wait. I wanted to have my ears pierced because all the other girls in my class had been allowed to have theirs done and were wearing pretty little earrings. My parents told me to wait until I was ten. Ten was a magic age for me. The day I was ten I realized a dream come true with golden earrings in my ears. Had I not been forced to wait, it would not have been as good. I was not responsible enough at five for getting my ears pierced and the responsibility of keeping them clean and just keeping up with the earrings. At ten I had learned that with the responsibility of having my ears pierced, I had to exercise care and put my earrings in the jewelry box. At sixteen, I secured my license to drive -- I had to wait until then, and it made the experience sweeter. I had learned that with every cause there was an effect. With a car entrusted to me, I had to be careful for another person.

"This is the same principle that should be exercised in the choice a woman has. She makes her choice before pregnancy. The experience of sex has responsibility. You know that, Steven. With every act there is a responsibility." She kept looking through the window at the darkness outside. *What was he thinking? Was he still there?* Yes, she knew he was. His presence was evident to her and a little unnerving. Had she been too explicit with this strange man?

"You've got it all figured out, haven't you, Annie. You will always be in control of your emotions. How many times have you had to exercise this choice, Miss Marrow?" he asked angrily.

Obviously she was inexperienced with men. The indignation that rose up in him made him want to take her in his arms and test her ability of control. He wanted to see if she knew what she was proclaiming. *Could she resist someone she loved? Who would she ever love enough to give herself to completely?*

Annie stood silently. His reaction was not surprising to her. They were on opposing teams. She had hoped to . . . what had she hoped . . . of course, he wouldn't be here if he was a Christian in the way she wanted to see him. He just knew God existed. But that was a start.

They heard a knock at the door, and Sally unlocked the door and, with basket in hand, began to clear the table. She looked from one to another sensing tension. *What was going on between the two? Had they enjoyed their meal?*

Annie came forward, walking directly in front of the solemn Steven. She attempted to help Sally at the same time smiling at her and saying, "Thank you, Sally and Steven, for making this a special memory. It was almost perfect."

She looked into Steven's eyes that were dark and blank, smiling at him as though nothing had happened.

Oh, how she gets under my skin, Steven thought. Her ability to turn everything into something for which to be thankful. He wanted to show her who was boss. He had never been so affected by a woman in his life. A shiver ran over him in defiance! *I promise before you leave here I will kiss those smiling lips!!* He promised himself.

While Sally busied herself with the cleaning and clearing of the table, Annie did what she could to help. Steven left the room as if it was too stifling for him. Annie only smiled to herself. She knew he was angry, but she hoped he would think about what she had said. It had all made sense. Some things were more precious from waiting, and being intimate with another person was one of those things. If one never had to wait for anything, she would have difficulty waiting to share herself in that way, also. Annie wondered why it mattered so much to her that Steven understand her opinion.

She had always tried not to offend other people, but it had never mattered so much as it did with this man she had known only a few hours . . . . . only a few hours?

CHAPTER FOURTEEN

Sunday morning dawned with the sun shining brightly. Julia and Andrew busied themselves getting ready for church. They had contemplated the decision thoroughly and decided that with the answering machine on they would risk it. Against all hopes there was not likely to be a call from Annie. The police were doing all in their power to follow every lead, and the couple felt they needed the strength from their fellow church members as well as the message from Pastor Thomason. Annie would certainly approve of their decision. She would desire to be in church, they both knew.

The close friends of the Marrows rallied around them and offered their help in any way that they were needed. The message was so helpful as Pastor Thomason spoke about how Christians face trials and problems to purify themselves and ultimately to glorify God in the result. This was what the Marrows desired in this trial. They asked the Holy Spirit to search their hearts as they knelt at the altar for prayer at the close of the service. They knew God was as near them at their own home, but there was just something more binding when they knelt before God at His house among the witness of His people.

Andrew took Julia's hand and led her back to the pew where they had been sitting and smiled a smile of assurance that all was going to bring God glory . . . . . no matter the outcome.

They returned home with the confidence that whatever trial they were to endure they had the strength of God to do so. The phone was ringing when they unlocked the door, and springing forward to answer it, Andrew learned that it was one of their foster children who had been in service and wanted to let them know that he had received Christ as his personal Savior the day before. He had met a young lady, who was a Christian, and she had witnessed to him time and again. He finally surrendered to Christ. Jody asked about Annie.

Andrew hesitated before telling Jody that Annie had disappeared and requesting that he and his fiancee pray for her safety and return. Jody promised to keep it quiet and pray.

Andrew could sense the hurt in Jody's voice. Jody had stayed in their home at the age of seven, and he and Annie had enjoyed being brother and sister very much. He often sent her little gifts and signed the card "Your loving brother." Annie had prayed for Jody to believe in Jesus as his personal Savior and would have rejoiced at the news. Andrew could see her in his mind's eye.

Her eyes would be glowing with excitement and she would say, "Another one of your children will be with us, Daddy." She would then say as if he were one of the family members present, "Thank you, Jesus, for loving us all."

Julia came downstairs just as Andrew was getting off the phone with Jody, and Andrew shared Jody's testimony with her.

"I wish Annie could know," Julia said. "She would be so happy. That is another prayer of hers answered." Julia smiled as she thought of Annie's simple prayers as a child for Jody, as well as all the children, that had been given foster care in their home.

She remembered on one such occasion when Annie was upset with Jody, and she had found Annie praying and laughed as she had said, "And God, if you can love Jody, change him so I can."

Now he was changed, but Annie had loved him with the love of Christ in spite of his aggravating ways, and that love prompted Jody to call wanting them to know of his salvation experience.

"God has a way of sending rainbows even in the cloud, Julia. Our life is cloudy with Annie's disappearance, but God knew we needed a rainbow of encouragement and sent the call from Jody. Another one in His fold. One by one, He is adding to His kingdom. Does that give us reason to rejoice even in this trial?"

"Andrew, I relinquished Annie to God completely, and I have had a feeling of peace. I am trying to keep my mind on God and less on the power of Satan, and the peace He promised has overtaken my heart."

"I know, honey." Andrew drew Julia into his arms, and they took comfort and strength from each other as God filled them.

CHAPTER FIFTEEN

Annie had dressed and was sitting in her favorite chair looking out the window. The sun was shining on the water that flowed at the foot of the slight incline, and it looked like diamonds sparkling beneath the sprawling limbs of the big oak. All was quiet in the Manor, and Annie thought about her own home. Would her parents be dressing for church? How she wished she could be there. She knew Pastor Thomason would bring a good message. She always felt so strengthened by his messages. He spent much time praying about what God would have him say to his congregation and studied to make it all he could from the human standpoint.

Annie's thoughts turned to Steven. He was probably back at the Good Samaritan by this time. Why did she feel such a loss? She missed him. He reminded her of Nathan in some ways. Yet, he was so determined, and Nathan could be reasoned with. Who would be her guard today? Would Jason take a turn at guarding her? She had not tried to get to know him as she thought he was someone else. What kind of day was ahead for her? Steven had brought pleasure in a bad situation. *Was that part of his charm? What kind of woman was he attracted to?* He had left that out of his summary of his dreams and likes and dislikes.

Steven had come by before she had retired for the night and told her he would be gone early in the morning before she would be awake, and that he had enjoyed the day. He seemed hesitant to leave and a little nervous to be there. *What was he thinking?* She had thanked him for everything, especially for the Bible and the special dinner. Annie was thinking about the way he avoided looking at her. Then she remembered him asking her if she was afraid Darlene would harm her. She had told him she wanted to see Darlene again when Darlene wasn't drinking.

He seemed surprised at this and had asked, "What do you have in common with her?"

Annie had replied, "Not a lot personality-wise, but we are both females and probably share some feelings and emotions."

Steven had grinned and shook his head as if he could not believe that. *Did he think she did not feel an attraction to the opposite sex? What had he called her "little ice maiden"? What had she to look forward to?* She would spend time today reading the Bible Steven had brought to her. She would tell Jason, if he came, that he could trust her to not try to escape.

Steven had left the Manor before seven. He had gone into the suite before he left and quietly opened her bedroom door. Annie had not locked it. This worried him a little as he knew Louis would be in and out of the house over the next couple of days.

Would Ramsey allow Louis to go back to the suite after he had learned of Louis's advances to Annie? It had not been so bad thus far, but knowing Louis's reputation, Steven did not feel at peace about leaving her. What was he thinking? She meant nothing to him. *But she did -- as a doctor, every human being was important. What had Annie said last night before the unpleasantness between them? She had said so much. For nineteen, she had some rather profound thoughts. She had said her dreams were no different from those of any other woman. Dreams of being catered to, treated special, be made to feel as if she were important to someone. Is that what women want from men? Some women required more than others to be made to feel special -- could that be because of having too much too soon? On what had Annie based her ability to wait -- to keep herself pure and wait for some man she would fall in love with? That dinner had meant a lot to her. Had she not thanked him over and over for it?*

He must put Annie from his mind and concentrate on his patients. She was safe and sound asleep when he stole a peek at her before he left. Sally would check on her. There was a possibility that Ramsey would release her before he returned to the Manor. Would he ever see her again if she was released? Would it matter? Of course, it would matter!! He did not get her address! She would not want to see him. Hey, Steven old boy, what is wrong with you, the old charmer? No woman has ever affected you. You could take them or leave them.

Sally came up with breakfast, and Annie was glad to see her.

"Good morning, Sally," she said with a big smile on her face.

"Good morning to you, Angel. You look like you slept for a change. I told Mr. Steven you needed some rest and to make sure you got some. That Louis kept you uneasy the night before, and that no-good Darlene can stir up trouble wherever she is. I made something special for you this morning -- fresh cinnamon rolls. I guess they are my specialty."

Annie hugged Sally and thanked her. "You have been so kind to me, Sally," Annie reminded her.

Annie looked under the soft pink napkin draped over the tray. The aroma of cinnamon reached her nose. "MMMMM--Sally, that smells great. Do you have time to stay a little while with me? Have you eaten?" Annie asked.

"Oh, yes, Angel. I have my breakfast early. But on Sunday I have some time between breakfast and lunch as we eat later, and that gives me a few minutes to read my Bible and relax." Sally looked at Annie with admiration.

"Could we read the Bible and pray together after I eat a bite, Sally?"

Annie asked excitedly. "That could serve as our church service."

"I'd like that." Sally felt privileged to be included. *How unselfish this little thing was! So unlike most young people of this age.* They did not want older people around, and most of the ones Sally had met did not read the Bible.

Annie finished her cinnamon rolls. They were tiny ones which showed the care with which Sally had made them. She drank her cup of coffee and glass of orange juice. Sally wrapped the remaining rolls in foil and left them on the table in hopes Annie would finish them off later.

Together they sat on the sofa as Annie opened the big black Bible and began reading from Hebrews twelve verse fourteen: "Follow peace with all men and holiness, without which no man shall see the Lord. Looking diligently lest any man fail of the grace of God, lest any root of bitterness springing up trouble you and thereby many be defiled."

Sally sat and listened to Annie read. Her voice was so sweet, and as she read it was evident she cherished the Word. *How could Dr. Ramsey do such a thing as hold her here if he had met her? But he had not gotten to know her. He would not understand such a girl.* Sally had not liked Mr. Meadows leasing the Manor to Dr. Ramsey, but Mr. Meadows did not know what was going on here, she was sure. How glad Sally was that Mr. Jason would be with Annie today, that is, if Mr. Steven could not.

"Sally, would you like to pray?" Annie was asking, catching hold of Sally's hand.

Sally began her prayer, "Dear God, our Father, thank you for this dear child. Keep her safe. Thank you for letting me meet her and for this sweet time communing with You together. Help Mr. Jason to be good to her and bless Mr. Steven while he is away. Save that no-good Louis and Darlene. Thank you for Jesus' love. Amen"

Annie looked at Sally and asked, "Is Darlene in the Manor today?"

"Angel, you don't have to fear that Darlene. Mr. Steven told Ramsey yesterday to keep her out of here," Sally answered, mistaking Annie's reason for asking about Darlene.

"I want to talk with her when she has not been drinking, Sally. She needs to be loved, and I want her to know I mean her no harm. I would like to be her friend. I don't want strife between us. The scripture reminded us to follow peace with all, and I want peace with Darlene as well as Louis, if possible," Annie said wishfully.

"They can only come in here if Mr. Jason is here. I heard Dr. Ramsey promise Mr. Steven that last night, myself." Sally looked at this girl in awe. She truly lived what she read as much as she could. That is the way we all should do, thought Sally. *I sometimes fail to do what I read about what God wants me to do. My life will never be the same after meeting this little angel.*

CHAPTER SIXTEEN

Sunday morning passed uneventfully after Sally left the suite. Sally busied herself with lunch which was always served around one o'clock at the Manor, allowing the guests to sleep late and breakfast leisurely. Annie had showered and dressed in the same dress she had worn the day before. She reasoned that she would prefer not to use more of the clothes provided than was necessary. There was no reason to worry about what she wore as her day would be spent in the suite.

How she longed to go for a long walk! The day was so lovely, and just to sit in the sun for a while would be so refreshing. She never saw anyone near the Manor from the window on the back. What harm would it be for her to be allowed to go for some exercise? She decided to ask Jason if he came into the suite. Perhaps he would take her plea to Dr. Ramsey. Better yet, she wished to talk to Dr. Ramsey herself to inquire about when he planned to release her.

She thought about her classes. How she hated to lose a whole semester of school! The expense was great, and costs were rising every year. Her parents had sacrificed to help her be able to go to school, and her working last year had given her a good start with money for college. She had hoped to make her grades work for her in securing a scholarship or two and relieve the financial pressure, but now -- if she did not leave here this week, she could be dropped from her classes, and that would not be good.

Her thoughts turned unexpectedly back to last night and Steven. He had been so congenial at times, almost tender, and then as their discussion progressed, he had become so angry.

Annie smiled as she remembered how he reacted to her suggestion that he was wearing a mask earlier in the day. She believed he was, and that he had been brought up to believe in God, with Godly parents. His reaction belied him. He had said that he was taught to go to church . . . that he did not like going to church. That was not really uncommon among youngsters at times.

Annie could never understand that as she had always loved church and the people there. She thought about Steven's family. He was the youngest of the three children. The only boy. A smile played on her lips; her eyes shone as she visualized his boyish face. No wonder he was spoiled -- she could imagine those bright blue eyes innocently pleading. *Who could have resisted him? That determination was perhaps already in his personality then. When did he decide to replace the honesty of his smile for a mask of deception? Was it to attract one particular female or anyone he desired at the moment?*

A knock sounded at the door just before the door was swung open. Jason came into the sitting room, tall and with much dignity in his appearance. He was dressed casually today, in olive Dockers and a multi-colored cotton sweater of olive, blue and navy. An olive-striped collar was visible at the neck of the sweater. He looked different in casual clothes than he did in the dark business suit of Friday. He had in his hand a selection of new magazines and something else.

"Hello, Miss Marrow." He smiled down at her from his obvious six feet. "You seem at ease today. You have adjusted well, I am told."

"What else could I do?" Annie replied with a little coolness. The nerve -- he had taken her hostage, and to make such a comment!

"I am sorry, I have tried to think of something to say to you from the moment I woke up this morning. I can understand your anger at me for tricking you into coming with me," he said lowering his head.

"Well, it was probably as much my fault as yours," Annie replied, checking her anger. "I should have asked your name instead of assuming." She must not let this place get under her skin if she was to be any kind of testimony of God's power in her life.

"I am the bearer of gifts for you," Jason said with a mischievous grin playing around his eyes as he pulled from underneath the magazines a neatly wrapped, flat package. He watched her expression intently. There was a note of surprise in her eyes and a sense of doubt as to whether she should accept.

"I do not like to take gifts from strangers," she said with caution.

"I gather this giver is not a total stranger to you, Miss Marrow. He has spent some time with you," Jason said mysteriously.

"But, how . . . .?" Annie let the question drop and reluctantly accepted the package from Jason's hands. "Please sit down while I open it, will you, Jason?" she said.

Was that fear in her voice, Jason thought. *Maybe she fears the package is from someone who wishes to harm her . . . perhaps he had made too much mystery of the little package.*

Annie carefully and slowly unwrapped the package; a strange light came into her big blue eyes. A tiny smile wrinkled her face as she lifted a stenographer's notebook and a slim silver pen. She turned the book over hoping to find the signature of the giver. She shook the pad but there was no card.

The puzzled look she turned on Jason, asked, "Did the person not wish to reveal his or her identity?"

Jason shrugged his shoulders and shook his head saying in this action that he did not know. "I was only asked to give it to you," he answered.

"Thank you, Jason. I shall enjoy writing while I am here," she said, and laying the notebook on the table by the window, carefully placing the pen beside it, she came back to the sofa.

"How have you been?" Annie asked sincerely.

Jason was taken by surprise at her contentedness and interest in him. She seemed so sincere in her inquiry.

He looked at her intently and replied, "Very well, and how about you?" He had never seen a girl with her ability to adjust at being held a hostage and be so at peace.

"Jason, I want you to know that I have forgiven you for the part you are playing in this situation. I am sure you have a reason which you think is valid. I could understand Louis and Darlene, perhaps; they both have not had the right kind of environment. That is my observation. I came to this conclusion because of the crude manner they both have. Of course, my observations could be wrong. You and Steven are different. I believe you both have been brought up to know better and have been educated well for your professions. I am having a hard time with your involvement."

Annie gave Jason a surprise of his life. *There was real concern for him in her voice. Amazing. And her knowledge of Louis and Darlene. How was she able to read people in this manner?*

"Miss Marrow, I have thought about what I have done. In picking you up and knowing of your mistaking me for this what was his name . . . Thornton? I have wished every waking moment that I had found the courage to risk saying, 'Forget it' to Dr. Ramsey."

"I work at the Good Samaritan as a physical therapist and have been closely associated with Ramsey for years. He has proven to be a good doctor. I thought at first that what he was doing was innocent. I could make a few bucks and feather my cap for promotion, and I saw no harm in the matter. He assured me there was no harm to come to you. Immediately after we had begun to leave Watertown, I was ashamed to be involved. Can you believe that?" Jason sat looking down at his hands that he kept interlocked as he flexed his fingers.

"Do you know when I will be released, Jason?" Annie asked.

"No, I'm sorry, I don't. I hated the idea of coming here today and facing you. But I was afraid that if I did not come, Louis would, and Steven and I discussed that at great lengths. We agreed to see this thing through and take our punishment for the involvement." Jason looked at her, and his eyes dropped again as if he did not want to see the sadness she was experiencing.

"Thank you, Jason, for being honest with me," Annie said and reached to touch his hand. "You do not need to guard me, I will not try to escape. I know this is your day off, is it not?" Annie looked earnestly at the man.

"Yes, it is," was all he could say without looking up.

"I am sure Dr. Ramsey would require you to stay in the Manor, but you could spend your time doing something more pleasant than guarding a hostage," Annie said with a laugh.

Jason got up from the chair, and his long lean body made a move to leave. Then he turned shyly.

"Miss Marrow, I know how lonely it is in here. Do you think we could have lunch together? I could ask Sally if she would mind preparing two trays instead of one." There was a convincing note in his voice.

"That would be very nice, Jason, if that is what you want. I must admit I enjoy the company of someone like you in a brotherly way," Annie said. If she was going to have a brother, she could think of no other one that she would rather he be like in some ways. Her thoughts went to the many "little brothers" that she had adopted -- the foster children. She smiled to think of the episodes with Jody. Where was he now? She was brought back to the present by the door opening.

Jason had gone. Annie walked to the chair beside the window, and sitting down she leaned her head on her hands, planting her elbows on the windowsill, and stared out the window. That scene would be indelibly imprinted on her mind. She saw the sun giving the lawn an appearance of gold. The grass had changed and the big oak formed patterns on the golden turf. Leaves of russet and orange shades swirled at the base of the tree. The blue-green stream flowed lazily. Annie spotted the first life she had seen on the view from the window; geese . . . or was it ducks . . . were swimming on the stream. Would they soon fly away? Would it get too cold for them? Would she ever go home?

She fought back tears that were forming in her eyes. She must think of something else. Jason . . . he was a quiet man. He had some unique ways about him. He had the capacity to succeed. He had said he was ashamed. That was a good sign.

Annie's attention was caught by the little notebook. She had almost forgotten about it. She had been so interested in Jason and his manner this morning that her thoughts concerning the notebook had been pushed aside. She reached and picked it up. She would write the thoughts she was having about Jason and their conversation. Opening the back cover, her eyes caught a note, written in a determined style, each letter formed with precision. It was a hard hand-writing to read, like that of a prescription, she thought and smiled with delight . . . Steven. The note read: "To be used for your desire to write. Take as needed. Can be refilled as often as needed to make you feel better. Signed: Dr. Steven Billups."

Annie felt warm all over as if she were being hugged. She would cherish this little gift always. A simple little notebook, yet it was a beautiful thought. Tears fell from her eyes and dropped on the bottom of the page. Why was she so touched, she asked herself. What a clever way to reveal who had sent the gift. Steven had shown how ingenious he was and how creative he could be. He must be a wonderful doctor with children, Annie thought. She held the notebook to herself and smiled, her thoughts transporting her far away from the situation she was facing.

After writing for a while, she bowed her head.

"Thank you, God, for loving me. You have given me hope today.

Help me to be a faithful follower of You. Thank you for letting my life touch these people that I would under ordinary circumstances never have known. Glorify Yourself in them."

CHAPTER SEVENTEEN

Steven had had a busy morning at the hospital. Children usually were brought in on the weekends in greater proportions. Many had been ill. This was the first break he had been able to take. Looking at his watch, he noticed it was five minutes to one. He was beginning to feel hungry. His thoughts went to another time he was hungry and the meal he had shared with Annie. He wished the evening had been pleasant until the end, but she could make him so exasperated.

He picked up his tray and proceeded through the cafeteria line. Several other doctors were filling the dining room and speaking to him as he chose his lunch. Now to find a table in an out of the way place where he could get lost for a while. He decided on one in the corner of the dining room. No one was sitting at the table next to his, so perhaps he could relax and think.

This was out of the ordinary for Steven as he was usually in the middle of everything and included by all his peers. He sat eating without really tasting the food, and his eyes looked as if no one was home. His thoughts were not at the hospital at the time. They were sorting through some things Annie had said to him last night. He had been so angry with her. Why did she make him so angry?

"Tony, Christina told me about that gem you bought for Annie," Nathan said. "Christina thinks that will impress her. You are really serious about her, aren't you?"

"I have never known anyone like her before," Tony replied.

Turning at these words, Steven saw Tony Harvey who had moved to the table near him. Steven had the expression of surprise and wonder. Annie who? he thought. He had not seen Tony with anyone.

Steven caught himself. What was wrong with him? There were other girls in the world who were named Annie. That was a common name.

He picked up his tray and started to move away from the table. He had been in med school with Tony Harvey, and their paths had crossed on a number of occasions. He had not been on the same floor with him here at the Good Samaritan and had seen Tony only at parties. The other guy he was not familiar with. Steven stopped by, reaching to shake hands with Tony.

"Hello, Tony," Steven said.

Tony stood up and began to introduce Nathan to Steven. Steven learned that Nathan was an accountant and worked with the Samaritan.

"I haven't seen you around," Tony was saying. "What field did you finally go into? Was it pediatrics? I do think I heard you paged for that floor," Tony said with sincere interest.

"Yes, that is it. And I have been paged quite a lot this morning," Steven laughed.

The question hung in Steven's mind, but he could not blurt out, "Who is Annie?" *Anyway, how would he explain knowing her if it was the little hostage? Was Tony her fiancé, and was he trying to impress her with a ring? Nathan had called it a gem. What was Nathan saying?*

"Would you join us, Steven?" Nathan was smiling and had the appearance of a very caring person.

"I would like to, maybe some other time. You guys enjoy your lunch. I need to get back to the floor." Steven wanted to get to know them. His reason was clearly personal. Perhaps tomorrow he would look for them.

"Oh, hello, Dr. Billups." A tall blonde girl dressed in a red wool suit came toward Steven. She caught him possessively by the arm; looking into his eyes, she turned on all her charm. Steven had been flattered by her attention at a party just last week and had promised to call her.

"You didn't call, Dr. Billups. I waited by the phone," she purred, still holding onto his arm as they walked to the swinging door.

"I have been very busy, Terri," Steven said.

"Can't you think of a better excuse than that? That is not the creative man I met just last week," the girl Steven had called Terri cunningly replied.

"I have been out of the hospital part of the time, and the case load is heavy." Steven had meant to call her, but she did not attract him as she had the night of the party. He had spent practically all the evening with her and found they had a lot in common.

"Could we have dinner together tonight?" she was asking. "I am on duty and will have some time for dinner around seven." She was quite persuasive.

Steven, knowing he was scheduled to have a break at that time, thought, *What would keep me from having dinner with her?* After all she had been in his thoughts after the party, and he had planned to call her. She was the type of girl he had been attracted to during the past few years.

"I think that can be arranged, Terri. I'll meet you here at seven," he said.

Terri smiled her most charming smile and tried to hold eye contact. Steven pushed the doors open and was gone.

Jason came up before one o'clock and brought the table -- the same table she and Steven had eaten on the night before. He put a white cloth on it and from a basket set the table. Annie stood by watching with amusement. She had offered to help, but he wanted to do it. Sally knocked on the door and came bustling in with a picnic basket full of food.

The succulent ham smelled so good, and Annie caught the fragrance of pineapple sauce. There was a congealed salad of raspberry jello with cream cheese and fruit topped with a garnish of dressing. The new potatoes cooked in sour cream looked simply mouth-watering. Green beans rounded out the meal.

As they sat down, Annie looked across the table and asked with interest, "Would you mind if we have a blessing on the food?"

Jason bowed his head, and Annie bowed hers. She began to pray, "Thank you, Father, for this food and thank you for the one who prepared it for us. Father, thank you for Jason and his offering to keep me company during this meal. In Jesus name. Amen."

Jason raised his eyes to Annie's. Then he began to fill her plate and his.

"May I call you Annie?" he asked shyly.

"Of course," Annie replied with a smile.

"I was brought up by my grandmother, and she is a Christian," Jason said tenderly. "She always prayed a blessing before meals. I did not think too much about it. I thought everyone did the same. As a child, she taught me to pray a little prayer, and when I outgrew it I did not pray anymore." Jason was trying to make conversation.

"Your grandmother sounds like a person I would like to meet," Annie said with sincerity.

"She died three years ago," Jason said.

"I am sorry." Annie reached over and touched his hand. "Do you have other family?"

"No, I was an only child. My parents died in a car accident when I was about two years old. My grandmother took me into her home, and I did not know of any relations other than her. It seems my grandfather had died before I was born. My grandmother sent me to college on a trust fund my grandfather had invested for any grandchild he had. I had thought I wanted to be a surgeon, but I decided a therapist was important, and that is what I am," he volunteered.

"I am sure you are a very good one, too," Annie said encouragingly.

The meal went well, and before it was over, Annie and Jason had learned a lot about each other.

Jason had expressed concern about his position in light of this involvement. Annie had not thought about what kind of trouble this could mean for him and Steven as well. She sincerely hoped all would end well for them all.

There was something about Jason that gave Annie hope, unlike Steven who was so set that his way was the only way. He could be so kind and caring yet so determined to prove his point. Jason, on the other hand, listened and thought about what he had heard and was easier to be made to feel ashamed. This could come from being brought up by his Christian grandmother. She had obviously loved him very much, yet somehow had not spoiled him. *What had Steven said about being spoiled by two sisters?* Jason had no one and needed a friend. Annie would try to be that friend.

They talked until late that afternoon, and no one interrupted them. Annie shared her faith with Jason. She did not want to push him, but when he started to leave the suite, she took a page from her notebook on which she had written some verses from the memory she had of a tract. She had kept this tract in her Bible to give to those who needed salvation or rededication.

After Jason left, Annie realized that in her enthusiasm to get to know more about Jason, she had completely forgotten about her desire to go outside for exercise. She had learned a lot about the shy young man. His grandmother had made a lasting impression on him even though he was resisting the things she wanted him to accept. Annie prayed that the verses she had shared would regenerate in his mind those things that he had been taught, and the Holy Spirit would use them to bring Jason to make a commitment to Christ.

Jason had been so tender today. He had not resented the idea of being with her but had brought the question up himself to have lunch there in the suite. Annie had been really surprised when Jason had openly, without coercion from her, told her about his grandmother being a Christian.

CHAPTER EIGHTEEN

Steven entered the dining room a few minutes before seven. His eyes scanned the room, and he caught sight of Terri, prim and proper in her white uniform. She had been Dr. Ramsey's nurse for about two years before she came to the Good Samaritan as Supervisor of Nurses. She had to work late on some occasions; she had informed Steven when they met at the party. He remembered her remark about her late hours at the hospital.

"That is not so bad. With you there, perhaps we can get together for dinner," he had said. She had smiled at him with that smile that told him she would be expecting dinners in the future when both were free.

He liked the idea. She was a new challenge. Women intrigued him, especially good-looking ones like Terri. The rumor that he set out to charm the women he met had been fueled by this intrigue he had for getting to know pretty faces. He had never been seriously interested in anyone for any period of time. There were always new challenges before him.

That is what he had thought when he met Annie. *How did her face come up in his vision?* She was definitely in a class by herself. He pushed

Annie from his mind as Terri smiled up at him from the most private table in the dining room.

"Dr. Billups, you are right on time!" Terri remarked. "I half expected you to be late or not show at all."

"Would I do that to a pretty young nurse?" he asked, and his blue eyes were shining excitedly.

"What are you eating?" Terri inquired. "I think I will stick to chicken salad; it looked really tasty."

"I think I will just pick up a BLT. I'm not extremely hungry, and those are my favorites." Steven answered. "I'll go get them for us," he volunteered.

The meal went well with Terri turning on all the charm she dared while being in the hospital cafeteria. She hoped this would lead to another date with this charming doctor. She must make a good impression. She had inquired about him and knew he liked a lot of the same things she did, and that they could have some enjoyable times together.

Steven was fighting hard to keep his thoughts on what was really happening around him. He looked across the table at the blonde woman, yet he was seeing another blonde with big blue eyes. The blue eyes he was seeing were so sincere. Nothing seemed hidden in them; they were all honesty and light.

He brought his thoughts back to the present with discipline. Terri was a pretty woman, he kept reminding himself. *Who was this Annie that Tony Harvey was trying to impress? Was it his Annie? Wait a minute* . . . . this thought had slipped into his mind unawares, and a chuckle escaped his throat at that moment.

"You are so preoccupied tonight, Dr. Billups," Terri was saying, turning her head to the side, looking very coy.

"I am sorry, Terri, and please call me Steven. I have heard 'Dr. Billups' today so much that it rings in my ears. I guess you could say I am home but my brain has gone out." He tried to make a joke, and they both laughed.

Steven knew he needed to be alone for a few minutes. He even regretted making this date. He was definitely not up to it. He sincerely hoped the cases would slow down long enough for him to get a little rest after dinner. He would check on the floor and steal away, if possible, for some time to himself. He made it through dinner and said goodbye to Terri at her floor.

Going up on the elevator, he was alone. His thoughts went back to the Manor. *What was going on there? Was Jason spending time with Annie, keeping her company to ease the hours? Would she enjoy Jason's company?* He was so glad Jason was there instead of Louis. Did he dare inquire into Tony Harvey's private life to find out who this Annie was in his life? When he saw Annie, if he ever saw her again . . . . . . the thought of not seeing her stabbed his heart. *Why did he feel so strongly about this strange girl? Did he dare ask her if she knew Tony Harvey?*

"Dr. Billups, please go to Room 214 in Pediatrics," a voice came over the intercom.

Steven entered the room as quickly as possible. His supervisor was there. Dr. Johnson looked up as he came in.

"I need to speak with you, Dr. Billups, as soon as you finish checking this young patient," he said and walked to his office on that floor.

Steven smiled at the little boy on the bed. "How are you, fella?" he asked with tenderness in his voice. He looked at the mother and father who were standing nervously nearby.

All the while Steven was reading the chart at the foot of the bed. A leukemia patient, the little boy had been to this hospital many times for chemotherapy before his cancer went into remission. The child was the only son of a Fort Drum soldier. With the child's immune system weakened by the leukemia, any type of virus or infection had to be taken more seriously than with other average, healthy children.

Steven put the chart in the rack and stepped beside the pale child. He began to feel the child's throat with gentle hands, looking into his eyes and smiling a smile of assurance.

"How long have you had a sore throat?" he asked the boy.

"A few days," he answered. "I just kept getting worse." The little boy's eyes were bright with excitement. Steven, sensing the boy's fright, turned to his parents.

"We will order a few preliminary tests, but I think it's a mild case of strep. He will need to be kept in the hospital away from other children for a few days." Steven felt comfortable with his diagnosis. The parents were relieved and relaxed.

"I noticed his temperature has been rather high, which is not uncommon. We will get that under control, and the rest and medication will do the job." Steven picked up the chart and left the room.

What did Dr. Johnson want with him? He wondered. *Had he heard about Dr. Ramsey's involvement with this hostage situation, and would he be calling Steven on the mat about his foolish part in it? Why had he ever gotten into this charade? Because he was the master of charades! Had he not been the one wearing a mask for so long? What,* he smiled to himself, all the while reprimanding himself for listening to a simple girl. He knew she was a very wise person. He knocked on the door of Dr. Johnson's office.

"Come in," Dr. Johnson said expectantly.

"The boy appears to have strep," Steven offered. "I have ordered the usual tests to see if my diagnosis is correct. Did you also check him, Dr. Johnson?" Steven inquired.

"Yes, Dr. Billups, and I concur with your opinion. I will get to the point at hand." Steven's heart beat rapidly against his chest as he waited breathlessly for the next words.

"Dr. Ramsey has requested that you be released tomorrow for an experiment he is doing. I told him you could leave the hospital for the twenty-four hours needed," Dr. Johnson stated.

Steven relaxed, but he was furious. He just hoped this mask would stay on to hide what was passing through his mind. The weight Ramsey carried was being used to his own advantage. *How could a doctor who had such potential get himself so worked up over an issue to the point of ruining his career and perhaps the careers of other men?*

"Dr. Ramsey said you would know of the experiment as you and he had discussed it before. He said you knew where to report by eight o'clock in the morning. Are you going to feel up to it after being on call all night here?" Dr. Johnson was asking.

Steven was standing as though in a trance, when suddenly he was brought back with Dr. Johnson's last question. *Would he be up to spending the day with Annie?* Nothing could keep him from it if Dr. Johnson approved.

"Yes, sir, I am very interested in seeing the outcome of this experiment," he answered. All the time he was wondering how Ramsey was going to get out of this untouched, or if he would. Would he be called to talk about this experiment he was supposedly doing?

"That will be all, Dr. Billups. By the way, I am impressed with your performance. You have a great future ahead. Be careful that you don't do anything to jeopardize it. Trust is a great part of being a good physician."

CHAPTER NINETEEN

Annie had been left to herself for much of the afternoon. She had done a lot of reading in the Bible that Steven had brought and had taken advantage of the time to put her thoughts on paper. It always helped her to understand herself when she could write down what was going through her mind.

Jason had been out of the room a long time. Annie walked to the window and looked across the lawn. The sun was casting elongated shadows across the burnished grass. Soon the sun would set and the night would take over, Annie thought. When Jason came back, she was going to ask to see Dr. Ramsey, she determined. He owed her an explanation, at least more than he had given on her arrival.

Her thoughts went back home to her parents. She knew that they would trust God in the matter, but she also knew that they would be anxious about her safety. She began to think about the arrangement that had been made here. Each man had taken his post of guarding her. She feared her encounter with Louis -- *what had Jason said about Louis not being able to come into the suite without he or Steven being there?*

A knock at the door brought Annie back to the time at hand. After unlocking the door, Jason came in.

"I am the bearer of an invitation to dinner in the dining room," he said. "It seems Dr. Ramsey wants the two of us to join him for dinner. I am not sure about the reason. But he asked me to inform you of his invitation, as he had several calls to make before he could meet us." Jason smiled at Annie in reassurance.

"What is this all about?" Annie asked.

"I don't know, but the change will do you good." Jason was gentle in his manner.

"Yes," Annie said absently, "it will give me an opportunity to speak with him also. I have wanted to ask him some questions all day. I had intended to ask you to have him come up here, but this will work out just fine." Annie smiled a knowing smile at Jason causing him to wonder what was going through her mind.

She is a complex young woman, he thought.

"What time should I be dressed?" was Annie's next question. It would be so good to see another part of the house, she thought. This suite had become monotonous as any place would when one had been locked in for several days.

"Be ready at 5 p.m. I better get dressed myself, for the big treat!" Jason laughed at his joke.

"I'll be ready, Jason," Annie said with determination. She had already begun to let her thoughts formulate ideas for the meeting with the great Dr. Ramsey.

Annie took a leisurely warm shower and applied her makeup with care. It would be good to get out of this suite if only for a few hours, she thought. She looked into the closet and chose a soft cream-colored silk dress that was embossed with pale pink roses and soft green leaves. The skirt fell softly around her perfectly shaped legs, and the hose she chose from the drawer was a soft taupe. There were cream heels to match the dress. As she brushed her shiny blonde curls, they shone with golden lights. She applied a light pink lipstick she had taken from the vast makeup kit provided for her.

Someone had spent a great deal of time assembling all the clothes, makeup and shoes for her stay here. Dr. Ramsey had made it as comfortable as he could to be holding her as hostage.

He was a strange person. He meant her no harm, but what his thinking was in holding her here, she must know. Annie took one more look at herself in the bathroom full-length mirror before going into the sitting room. This dress was perfect for her complexion. The pink of the roses brought color to her cheeks. Annie thought this was probably the most expensive dress she had ever worn.

Preparation had to be made for the meeting with Dr. Ramsey. She did not want to go into it just half prepared. Picking up the big Bible, she turned to Isaiah 41:10 and began to read aloud: "Fear thou not; for I am with thee."

Annie was sitting with her back to the room, looking out the window. This had become special to her. "Thank you, God, for that promise," she whispered. She was unaware that anyone else was listening, as she did not hear the lock and the door open softly.

She continued, "Be not dismayed; for I am thy God; I will strengthen thee; yea, I will help thee: yea, I will uphold thee with the right hand of My righteousness."

"Oh, Father, I am trusting You," she said in earnest. She continued to read, "Behold, all they that are incensed against thee, shall be ashamed and confounded: they shall be as nothing; and they that strive with thee shall perish." Annie bowed her head and hugged the Bible to her. She did not know how long she sat there communing with her God and Father.

The person at the door was as one frozen to the spot. After some time elapsed, he turned and quietly pulled the door shut.

Annie, after some time of praying and thinking about what she must do tonight, laid the Bible on the table and moved over to the sofa to wait for Jason's return. She began to hum a song that had been a favorite of hers for sometime. She had heard a group that had come to her church sing this song. The words spoke of Jesus being as close as the mention of His name. She would carry that with her to dinner. It could be consoling to her. She was a little nervous, and at the same time she was anticipating her time with Dr. Ramsey.

Jason's knock and entry came, and Annie gave him a big smile. He looked rather handsome -- not in the same way as Steven, she thought, but he was a good guy. She hated that he had given in to the pressure of Ramsey and found himself in this mess. Jason showed his approval of her appearance.

"You will knock Ramsey out cold," he laughingly said as if he wanted to see the doctor's reaction to his hostage.

"Thank you, Jason." She walked toward him and he reached for her hand as he led her out of the room and slowly down the massive staircase. Annie surveyed the Manor with a new light. She remembered that Friday and her bewilderment as Jason led her up these same stairs. The fear that had gripped her heart had been taken away by the Holy Spirit, and she had to admit her stay here had some pleasant moments. Her mind strayed to the time spent with Steven. She took a deep breath, and the fragrance of roses drifted up the stairs.

Looking into the dining room, she saw the origin of that scent. A large arrangement of the most beautiful variegated roses adorned the table. There was a white lace runner down the center of the huge mahogany table. The table was polished to a shine that denoted much time. There were matching lace placemats, and ivory china embossed with pink apple blossoms glistened at each place setting.

A smile spread across Annie's face, and she squeezed Jason's hand as she looked up at him. He thought how like a little girl she looked. He had always thought how nice a little sister would be. He was beginning to think of Annie as a little sister. Funny that he could be so at ease with her today. He remembered how he had felt on that Friday. He had later discovered that his feelings were that of amazement, causing him to be shy with her.

Dr. Ramsey came out of the study at the time Annie and Jason reached the third step from the foyer. Jason was fighting to keep the smile of "I told you so" from spreading across his face. Dr. Ramsey could not cover the surprise that he was experiencing. Annie was lovely and radiated as she seemingly floated down the last three steps. She spoke before the doctor had time.

"Hello, Dr. Ramsey," she said and extended her hand to shake his. Her action took Ramsey totally by surprise, as he took hold of the delicate hand extended.

"You look lovely, Miss Marrow," he said, obviously being shaken by her attitude as well as her appearance.

"Well, you will have to take the credit for that, Dr. Ramsey. This is the most beautiful dress I have ever worn. You really have good taste. And you obviously knew my coloring and size. I would say you are definitely thorough in your planning," Annie said sweetly but sincerely.

Ramsey seemed to be rattled by her honesty and sincerity. Whatever he had expected he had definitely not seen in Annie. He led her into the dining room trying to muster some composure on the way. After seating Annie on his right and Jason on his left, he took the seat at the head of the table.

"I wanted to take this opportunity to talk with you, Miss Marrow. I felt what I had to say could best be said in pleasant surroundings," Dr. Ramsey said, a little nervously.

"Of course, Dr. Ramsey, I am happy you did. It is odd that all day today, I felt it necessary that I speak with you. I had thought of asking Jason to make an appointment with you today, and when your invitation came, I was very pleased." Annie smiled at him, letting her eyes look directly into his dark ones.

Jason lowered his head, fighting a smile as he watched the interplay of these two opposite people. Annie was prepared for anything, he thought. He remembered her reading the Bible. He would not take anything for that experience. It had brought back memories of his grandmother. When she needed strength she knew where to go. Hearing Annie read that verse from Isaiah pierced my heart, thought Jason.

Ramsey had to regroup before he went on. The conversation was not going as he thought it would. He expected to be totally in control, and each time he opened his mouth, very gently and kindly Annie took possession of the ball, so to speak.

"I hope your stay has brought you no harm, Miss Marrow; your being brought here was not done with any intention of harm coming to you," Dr. Ramsey said, looking at Annie as he sipped a glass of wine.

"I have been treated very kindly by most people here, Dr. Ramsey," Annie replied. "But I have been harmed by being brought here. I have gotten behind in my college classes because of my absences. My parents have suffered grief and worry over their only child. The police have, in all likelihood, been called in, causing them to be taken from more pressing crimes. Much harm has come from your action. The only unpleasantness I have personally suffered has been fear of certain individuals and the confinement to the suite. The intimidation of being held against my will angered me until I realized I was needed here." Annie concluded her statement to Dr. Ramsey's puzzlement.

"My one question is what has been accomplished concerning your plans, Dr. Ramsey?" Annie asked boldly.

"Miss Marrow, you were brought here to deter your father from pursuing this plan to complete the pregnancy center and placement home for women. I felt by causing a crisis in his family he would not be able to function properly and would have to delay his plans. Thereby, the permit would expire on the building before it could be started and the property would revert back to the original heirs. I was wrong, as he never missed a meeting and the building was started in spite of his only daughter dropping off the face of the earth. What kind of father do you have, Miss Marrow?" Dr. Ramsey was angry as he saw his plan was failing.

"I have a devoted, committed father, Dr. Ramsey," Annie offered.

"He did not seem to be as worried as you make him to be," Dr. Ramsey observed.

"I am sure he was anxious in his own way, Dr. Ramsey. You see, my father had already counted the cost of involvement in this project before he committed himself to it. He may not have thought about the abduction of his daughter as the opposition's strategy to block the helping of these women, but he knew there was strong opposition to his offering an alternative to women who otherwise would be taking the life of their unborn children. He feels strongly that something needs to be done, and my mother and I were aware of the cost that our family might have to pay for him to follow the Lord in doing whatever God laid on his heart to do," Annie boldly answered.

At this time, Sally and Rosena came in with the first course of the evening meal. A delicious bowl of piping hot Veloute of Asparagus was set before Annie. The aroma was making her hungry in spite of the heated conversation that had transpired between Dr. Ramsey and herself. Jason had kept quiet during this discussion but had admired the boldness of Annie in standing up to the doctor. Annie smiled up at Sally as she left the room.

"This smells wonderful," Annie said admiringly, looking first at Dr. Ramsey and then to Jason. She bowed her head and for a moment all was silent.

Jason knew she was thanking God for the food and the strength He had given her to stand up to Ramsey. Ramsey looked up under his lashes as he began to spoon his soup. When he raised his head and noticed Annie, he had a puzzled look on his dark face.

"Sally is a good cook," Jason said. "She told me she had been with the Manor for quite a long time."

"Yes, she is a good cook," Dr. Ramsey said. "She is an unusual person also."

"Do you own the Manor?" Annie asked Ramsey.

"No, the man who owns it was a patient of my father. He calls me from time to time for consultation, and he leased it to me while he is in Europe," Ramsey said.

The rest of the meal went smoothly, and as they were having a cup of coffee after the meal, Annie asked, "Dr. Ramsey, you gave me the impression that your plan to stop the development of the clinic has failed. Does that mean that you are going to let me return home?" Annie came right to the point.

"I do plan to release you soon, Miss Marrow," Dr. Ramsey said, contemplating just what his plans were.

"I would like my parents to be assured of my safety. Could you do that since you are aware that my absence has nothing to do with stopping my father's ministry?" Annie asked.

"I am in no hurry to leave now as I feel I am needed here," Annie stated. "Besides, if you hold me a lot longer, I will incur too many absences and have to drop my college classes anyway."

Ramsey looked at her strangely. *What is she talking about?*

"You say you are needed here, Miss Marrow. In what way are you needed?" Ramsey asked, perplexed.

"Dr. Ramsey, you brought me here, and I was angry to be held against my will, but while I have been here, God has shown me that had you not brought me here I would never have met some people any other way. I trust the lives of these people have been touched by knowing me just as my life has been touched by knowing them. You know, that is what life is all about." She looked across the table at Jason.

Their eyes met, and Jason could see she was as sincere as she could be. This was no ploy, but she actually believed what she was saying. Jason knew his life had been touched by knowing her. Would Ramsey's life be changed by knowing his hostage?

For the first time, Jason saw Ramsey speechless. The doctor did not understand this little woman. She was so simple and yet so wise. *Is that what it is like to trust Jesus?* The little hostage had taken them hostage.

"Have you thought that the police could link you with the kidnapping, Dr. Ramsey?" Annie asked.

"Yes, the thought has crossed my mind, but I could claim you weren't kidnapped. You have become good friends with those who took you and have been guarding you." He was grasping for something to rectify his mistake.

"That is true. I do not wish any harm to come to you, Dr. Ramsey, because of this event. I certainly hope these young people you have involved in your scheme will come out unharmed professionally," Annie said calmly, realizing she was in control of the conversation.

"I am concerned about one thing. If the police have been called in, and I'm sure they have been, will we be able to get you off some way?" Annie questioned.

"If charges are pressed . . . . " Ramsey started.

"What good would it do us to press charges against you, Dr. Ramsey?" Annie asked. "Our intention is not to put you in prison or punish you -- just to be able to share our viewpoints about what you are involved in with the abortion clinic. Would you allow me to do that now?" Annie asked permission.

"What can you tell me that I do not already know, Miss Marrow? Do you forget that I am a doctor?" Ramsey asked.

"Do you believe that the Bible is God's Word, Dr. Ramsey?" Annie quizzed.

"Well, I believe it's supposed to be," he answered.

"But you are not sure it is?" Annie probed.

"I was brought up by parents who believed in God, Miss Marrow," Ramsey answered emphatically.

"But you, do you believe in God? It is not enough that you had parents who did, you must decide for yourself," Annie said.

"What has that to do with the abortion issue?" Ramsey asked.

Jason thought as he listened to the conversation. *Ramsey, you have asked just the question she wanted you to.* He could hardly keep from smiling as he saw Annie with a flicker of light shining in her big blue eyes.

"God's Word talks about the forming of a tiny human being before anyone knew the little human existed," Annie said reverently. "David in the Psalms said God knew him when he was in his mother's womb, when his substance was hid, he was made in secret, yet God saw him and he was recorded in the book -- even all his members or body parts were recorded before there was even any substance made. Can you imagine all the little babies that have been taken from their mothers' wombs recorded by God in His book of memories? It is awesome to me. God's thoughts are precious unto these little ones. Do you think you have a right to take one of these little ones that God is forming for His glory in some woman's womb and destroy it, Dr. Ramsey?" Annie bowed her head fearing his answer.

Jason held his breath. Ramsey was white around his mouth, and anger flared in his eyes. He pushed his chair back from the table and left the room. Jason knew Ramsey had to leave for fear of what he would do. There was silence at the table as they both sat motionless for a time.

CHAPTER TWENTY

Jason had taken Annie back to the suite after dinner. They sat on the sofa and talked for some time. They had heard nothing else from Dr. Ramsey. Around ten o'clock, Jason left Annie with a promise to see her before he left the Manor the next morning. Annie reminded Jason that she wished to see Darlene and Louis before she was released.

"I will tell Dr. Ramsey before I leave the Manor in the morning," Jason had promised.

With this he had left Annie for the night. Annie thought about how good it would be to be back home. Dr. Ramsey had given his word that she would be released soon. She thought about his surprise at the fact that he had not been successful in his effort to hinder her father from accomplishing his goal to build the center. Annie smiled to think her father had trusted God in this crisis. She felt he would and had prayed that God would give him comfort in this time. The faith she had lived with during her nineteen years had been evident during her absence, even though her parents were grieved.

She slipped into bed and read the Bible until she dropped off to sleep. Her last thought and prayer was for Jason and Steven. *Where was Steven tonight? He was working, but what kind of night was he having?*

Jason had been touched by the conversation with Annie, and a smile crept across his face as he remembered her confrontation with Ramsey. Ramsey was startled by her wisdom and boldness. She had had the upper hand all the way tonight.

As Jason slipped into his bed, he began to run over in his mind the way she had asked him if he had ever received Christ into his heart. He knew he had gone to the altar as a little boy and committed his life to God. But as he grew into the teen years he had left God out of his life. And then there was college -- God was not a part of his life there.

His grandmother had trusted God for everything, and when she died he remembered her saying to him, "Jason, remember when I'm gone, you will not be alone. Jesus will always be with you."

He had thought that was so elementary to say to a grown man. Then she had said, "I trust you will commit your life to Him, soon."

He had smiled at her through the tears that had been in his eyes and said, "Yes, Grandmother. Don't worry." Those were the last words they had exchanged. He had been asked to leave the intensive care ward, and shortly after that the doctor came to give him the news that his grandmother had died.

Jason had taken the sheet of paper Annie had given him earlier from his pocket and laid it on the bedside table. He picked it up and began to read:

"All have sinned and come short of the glory of God."

"The wages of sin is death, but the gift of God is eternal life."

"But God commended His love toward us in that while we were yet sinners, Christ died for us."

"If thou shalt confess with thy mouth the Lord Jesus, and believe in thine heart that God hath raised him from the dead, thou shalt be saved."

"Whosoever believeth on Him shall not be ashamed."

The tears streamed down Jason's cheeks. He thought of his grandmother and of the girl next door. They were alike. They both knew what he needed. His grandmother had told him time and again, and now this very girl that he had so easily taken as hostage had written it out for him. He looked at his watch. *Was she asleep?*

Jason knelt beside the bed and in his simple way asked God's forgiveness. Confessing his sin of unbelief, he then asked Jesus, the Lord of his grandmother and of Annie Marrow, to be his Lord. He was so happy and felt so free he wanted to tell someone.

Jason pulled on his robe and went into the corridor to the suite next door. He listened at the door for a sound. All was quiet. Cautiously he turned the lock and opened the door slightly. He would call to her, he thought.

"Annie, Annie," he called, his voice almost a whisper at first.

Annie, hearing someone faintly calling, listened again. Was she asleep or was someone at the door? *Who could it be?* She grabbed the robe she had laid on the chair beside the bed and opened the door a crack, making sure before she went into the sitting room.

"May I come in?" Jason whispered.

"Come on in, Jason." She was puzzled as to why he had returned to her room this late. Surely it was something urgent, she thought.

"Annie, I am sorry to wake you, but I needed to talk to someone. You can understand what I am going to say," Jason faltered. "I have watched you all day, and then tonight when you confronted Ramsey with such boldness and determination, I was touched. Your conversation with me and just your attitude about life and about God has stirred up some feelings and brought to surface some truths that my grandmother taught to me both in word and in her very actions. When I read the verses you had written for me, I knew I had to ask forgiveness for leaving God out of my life and for the things I have done against Him. Annie, I prayed and gave my heart to God. He has lifted that burden and freed me to live for Him." Jason looked down at his trembling hands, a little nervous at his confession.

"Oh, Jason," was all Annie could say at the moment. She ran across the room and put her arms around him as a sister would a brother. "Now we are real brother and sister," she said smiling as tears rolled out of her big blue eyes and crept down her pretty face. "Now you have made the angels rejoice and your grandmother happy over your return to God."

"Do you think so?" Jason asked sounding almost like a little boy.

That is what salvation is all about, thought Annie, we must come as simple as little children.

"You know, Annie, I was young when I felt God wanted me to give my heart to Him," Jason began. "I gave my heart at the time, the heart of a little boy, but then when I grew up I tried to forget about ever committing to Him. I kept pushing Him away. I was miserable but did not realize how miserable until I saw how happy you were in your faith."

"I knew you appeared puzzled when you saw me content to be here. I admit I would rather be home with my parents, and I know they are worried, but, Jason, when I was reading about Paul and how while he was in prison he wrote to the Philippians and told them he had learned to be content in whatever state he was in . . . I knew . . . I had it good compared to what Paul was enduring . . . I then began to pray that God would be glorified through my being here. Tonight, God is being glorified through your rededication to Him. Now you must help me to pray for the others involved. Will you do that?"

"Annie, your boldness and sweetness with Dr. Ramsey was also glorifying to God, I am sure," Jason reminded her.

They prayed together holding hands, and then Jason said goodnight, promising that they would not lose touch even after this ordeal was over.

Knowing her parents' phone number was unlisted, Annie wrote her name and number on a piece of paper and tucked it in his hand. Jason left the suite with a determination to do something that might put him in jail. He knew it had to be done as soon as he could get away from the Manor.

Before going to sleep, he read the verses over and over again. Then he folded the piece of paper along with the telephone number and put it into his coat pocket. He would treasure that little piece of paper forever.

CHAPTER TWENTY-ONE

Annie had slept well after the visit from Jason. She felt the purposed imprisonment had accomplished much. Jason had been so sincere. She had been so happy at the thought of him surrendering to Christ. *If only Steven could be reached.* She wondered if someone would come to guard her today. She knew Jason would return to work at the Good Samaritan. She hoped to see Darlene and Louis before her release, but most of all she wanted to see Steven. It had seemed such a long time since they had spent the day together. She relived the time they had been together.

Returning to the window and looking out on the back lawn, Annie picked up the Bible. How much consolation this Book had meant to her! How thankful she was to Steven for bringing it up on that Saturday. Her eyes turned to the stenographer's notebook. Her many thoughts were written in that plain little notebook. A page from that book had been used by God to bring Jason to rededicate his life to God. It took so little on our part, she thought, to trigger the heart to turn to the prompting of the Holy Spirit.

Reading from Psalm 119, Annie noted how much the psalmist referred to the word of God, and its power. Over and over the importance of keeping the Word was emphasized. Verse 133 caught her eye: "Order my steps in thy word; and let not any iniquity have dominion over me."

"Dear Father, I claim this verse today. I do not know what I will be confronted with, but keep me in Your sweet will. Let my life be glorifying to You," Annie prayed.

Going into the bathroom, she showered and dressed for the day. She chose a dark navy and red plaid skirt and a beautiful long-sleeve cotton sweater in red to match. Embroidered on the front of the sweater were navy designs edged in gold to match the skirt. Her blonde hair was shining this morning. The big blue eyes held a special twinkle.

Annie was thinking about her talk of last night with Dr. Ramsey. He had promised her soon release. *Would it be today?* The anticipation of going home caused her much joy, yet would she ever see Steven again? Jason had told her he would like to see her again. Would Steven feel the same way? She knew they did not run in the same circles. Steven had told her how he felt about church and Christians.

A knock sounded at the door. It was early as Annie had been so anxious to be up and dressed this morning. Could this be Sally with her breakfast? She usually did not bring it until after eight o'clock, and it was only a little after six. Annie turned expectantly as the lock clicked and the door opened. It was not Sally but Darlene.

"Dr. Ramsey said you wanted to see me," Darlene said calmly. Annie had never seen her this calm. She always stormed in and began to make trouble.

"Hello, Darlene," Annie said with a smile. "Please come in and sit down."

"I was told I was to apologize to you for my behavior," Darlene began without looking at Annie. She was looking at her clenched fists in her lap. Her long auburn hair was fluffing out around her pretty face.

Annie looked at her with compassion. She could really be a pretty

139

girl, thought Annie. Darlene had appeared to take extra care in applying her makeup this morning, and the green top she wore over the khaki pants brought out the brilliant green of her eyes.

"Everything is all right between us as far as I am concerned, Darlene. I want to be your friend," Annie said sincerely.

"You do?" Darlene looked at her as if she had a hard time believing that.

"Yes, I do," Annie answered.

"You aren't mad at being held here against your will?" Darlene asked with wonder in her eyes.

"It was not the most pleasant thing to have happen to me, but I have met some nice people since I came here, people I would not have met any other way," Annie replied.

"You are talking about Jason and Steven, I guess." Darlene said this with a questioning look on her face.

"And you," Annie said, omitting Louis because she feared a reaction from Darlene. She wanted to keep Darlene calm until she had the opportunity to cement their relationship. Darlene was having a hard time believing Annie could want to be friends.

Annie did not want to do anything to jeopardize the progress they were making.

"Why would you think of me as a friend? We are so different," Darlene said defensively.

"There are some things that are different about us, Darlene, but we are so alike in other ways," Annie said with conviction.

"I guess I don't see how we are alike, but I certainly see how we are different," Darlene said sarcastically.

"What do you see that is different about me?" Annie asked.

"You are a fanatic and look down your nose at people like Louis and me," Darlene accused.

"I am sorry that you got that impression from me, Darlene. I did not intend to give the impression that I look down my nose. You are a lovely person with your pretty auburn hair and most startling green eyes. Why would I not like you?" Annie asked, trying to probe into Darlene's mind.

"Well, for one thing, that father of yours is against people like me, and you are too." Darlene was grasping for straws.

"You are wrong there, Darlene. My father loves women who need help and is trying to provide a way of helping them. Do you think because he is against abortion that he is against you? Why would you think that?" Annie asked, trying to bring out the real issue.

"I had an abortion. He makes that a bad thing to do. It was all I could do. I don't have anyone to care for me except Louis," Darlene said.

"Just because you had an abortion does not mean my father or I do not like you. We do like you, and that is why he wants to give girls like you an alternative to having an abortion. He does not want to be judgmental of you. He wants to help you any way he can to have a happy life. You know, Darlene, there is someone else who loves you," Annie said, smiling at Darlene.

"Who?" Darlene asked looking at Annie in amazement.

"God," Annie said simply.

"God?" With this Darlene laughed in derision. "How could He love me?"

"I don't quite know how He loves any of us, Darlene, you see none of us deserve His love. I don't deserve His love, my father doesn't deserve His love, but he loves us just the same. He left us a letter to tell us that He loved us so much that He sent His son to die to take our punishment so that we might be saved from the punishment of hell, that we deserve," Annie said with love in her voice.

"What do you want from me?" Darlene asked uneasily.

"I just want to share God's love with you, Darlene," Annie said. She picked up the Bible and read: "All have sinned and come short of the glory of God."

"Did you hear that, Darlene? We all have sinned, and therefore we all need a Savior."

"What did you do? Did you have an abortion too?" Darlene asked.

"I did not have to do anything, Darlene -- just be born into a sinful state because of Adam's sin. Adam and Eve, the first man and woman, sinned and plunged the whole world into sin. I came to the realization that because I was unable to keep from sinning, I needed someone to stand before God in my behalf, and Jesus, who came and lived on this world as a man, never sinned so He could die for me and stand before God in my stead, a perfect sacrifice.

"I needed someone to stand between me and God and I received Jesus as my Savior. In doing so, I pledged my love to Him, and He became the Lord of my life. I am His and that is why you think I am a fanatic. I do not belong to myself anymore but belong to Him. Because of what He has done for me, I want to keep myself pure and blameless in His sight. I don't want to hurt Him," Annie explained.

"But I am not pure, and I have made a mess of my life," Darlene said excitedly.

"It doesn't matter how big a mess you have made, Darlene, Jesus wants to love you, and He will if you will let Him," Annie said with persuasion in her voice.

"I don't know," Darlene said. A struggle was going on in Darlene's life -- a struggle between darkness and light.

"What do you have to lose?" Annie asked.

"I could lose Louis," Darlene said. "He would not like a goody-two-shoes."

"Are you so sure of Louis's love, Darlene?" Annie asked, knowing she was treading on thin ice.

"What do you mean?" Darlene became angry and defensive.

"I know human love can fail us sometimes, but God's love never fails," Annie said with calmness in her voice.

Darlene was thinking about what Annie had said. She was undecided. She looked at Annie and wished that she had her calmness and ability to find contentment, yet could she leave the old life behind? Annie had the support of a family. Darlene realized she had nothing.

Annie walked over to the table at the window, picked up a piece of paper and folded it neatly making a type of envelope. She had worked on this yesterday. It was all she had to give to Darlene. She hoped it would mean something to her after they were apart. She had prayed that God would help Darlene to see His love for her.

Annie wanted to keep in touch with Darlene after leaving the Manor. She did not know how Darlene would feel about that.

"Darlene, I want you to have this little gift from me. I have written you a letter inside and enclosed my address. Dr. Ramsey has promised that I will be released soon, and I want you to know that I believe God has allowed me to be brought here so I could get to know you and have you for a friend. Will you be my friend?" Annie pleaded.

Darlene was surprised. She took the little envelope, turned it over and read what Annie had written on the front, "Open when you are lonely and need a friend." That could be most anytime, Darlene thought. What should she say to this girl? Was she sincere? Does she really want to be my friend, Darlene wondered. She seems sincere enough. She was a strange girl.

"You really want me for a friend?" Darlene asked.

"Yes, I do," Annie said convincingly and smiled at Darlene.

A knock sounded at the door, and the lock turned. Sally came in with Annie's breakfast tray. She looked first at Annie and then with alarm in her eyes at Darlene. What was that no-good doing in here, she questioned in her mind. The look on Annie's face was radiant. Whatever had been going on, God was working through it.

Sally placed the tray on the table beside the door and said, "Good morning. It's going to be a beautiful day, Miss Annie."

"Yes, it is, Sally," Annie said smiling.

Darlene turned and left the room clutching the little homemade envelope in her hand. She seemed unaware of anyone else around her as she closed the door leaving Sally and Annie inside.

CHAPTER TWENTY-TWO

Steven had finished up at the hospital and was coming out of the elevator when he saw Jason. Anxious to hear from the Manor, he caught up to him and began to ask questions. Jason had told Steven of Ramsey's conversation with Annie and how he had left the table in anger.

"You look happy this morning," Steven remarked, wondering what had made such a difference in Jason. *Could it be he has fallen for Annie?* That would not surprise Steven if he did. She was so unusual.

"I am very happy," said Jason, smiling. "I wish I had time to tell you all about it, but I'm due in Room 318 immediately. I'm running a little late. Perhaps, when you return from the Manor, we can talk. I have made a decision I know is right for me. I hope I can soon put that decision to rest."

Jason seemed to have more confidence this morning, which was leaving Steven confused.

"We will have some time tomorrow maybe," Steven said, hating to leave this question unanswered with Jason.

As Steven drove to the Manor, his thoughts kept returning to Jason. *What was making such a difference in him?* Oh, well, he would have to wait about that until they could get together. How glad he would be to get this Ramsey thing behind them, or would he? . . . . Annie would return to her home . . . and what then? Would she ever want to see any of them again? To think of not seeing her brought a pain of regret to his heart. *What was it about her?* He remembered how during the night, as he was between patients, she had been constantly in his thoughts. He shook his head as if he was trying to erase the thought of her.

It was a beautiful morning, and the drive to the Manor was a relaxing one. The day was crisp and cool but not as cold as it had been. It could be a great day for a picnic . . . a picnic with Annie. That would be fun. He could see her now. She seemed to love the outside. He had watched her often as she looked longingly out the window. That was an idea!

The maroon Camry circled into the drive and stopped at the door of the Manor. Steven gathered his briefcase and a bag from the backseat and rushed up the steps. He unlocked the door and stepped into the foyer. Should he go see Annie first? His desire was to rush up the stairs to her, but he decided to try to see if Ramsey had left instead. Ramsey would be in the study if he was here.

Steven knocked on the door. There was no answer. Dr. Ramsey must have left for the hospital. There was just one thing to do, thought Steven. He entered the study and dialed the hospital. The switchboard answered, and Steven was connected with Dr. Ramsey shortly. After some time and a lot of persuasion, he hung the phone up and, closing the door behind him, started up the staircase taking two steps at a time.

He hesitated outside the door to Annie's suite, catching his breath. He knocked on the door before he inserted the key into the lock.

Annie was sitting on the sofa, looking at a magazine he had sent to her by Jason. A big smile spread across her face as Steven came into the room. The sight of him caused the blood to rush to her face. A thrill of excitement was in the air.

"Hello, Annie," Steven said with a smile. There was a twinkle in his eyes that told Annie he was glad to see her. Had she forgotten how mad he was when he left her?

"Hello," she said with shyness, fearing he would see how very happy she was to see him again. What was wrong with her? She had never been so happy to be in a man's presence before.

"I have a big surprise for you!" Steven exclaimed in a boyish manner. His eyes were looking deep into her big blue eyes, and he liked what he saw. Was she aware of the effect she was having on him?

"You have already surprised me. Thank you for the notebook. I have put it to good use. You were so kind to think of it." Annie was trying to hide her excitement at his being there.

"But this is something I think you will really like," he answered, almost bursting to reveal his plans to her.

"What? Am I going home?" She wanted to go home, but the thought of not seeing Steven again brought a cloudiness to her eyes.

Steven noted this and wondered what she was thinking. He came close and sat on the sofa beside her. He turned to face her, and his hand ran across the back of the sofa barely touching her blonde curls. How he would like to run his hands into that golden mass!

"How would you like to go on a picnic down by the stream today? Isn't that the next best thing to going home?" Steven asked, smiling with a feeling of victory. Dr. Ramsey had objected at first, and then Steven had assured him they would not be seen and he would take care that they weren't.

"Oh, Steven!" Annie smiled and, reaching out, touched his arm with her delicate little hand. "Are you serious? I know it's a gorgeous day out there. I got up early this morning to look out on the lawn and wished to be able to run in the fresh air," Annie cried excitedly.

Steven wished they could stay as they were, her hand reaching out to touch him. He was being silly. No girl had ever had this effect on him before.

Reluctantly, not really wishing to leave her for one moment, he said, "I'll go see if Sally can pack us a basket of lunch. You get ready and I'll be back soon."

They both stood up, and Annie caught hold of Steven's arm. With a radiant smile on her face, she said, "You think of the nicest things, Steven."

Steven left the suite taking two steps at a time and almost colliding with Sally as she came around the landing.

"Mr. Steven, you're in a big hurry this morning. What's the matter with you?" Sally looked at him as though she thought the house was on fire.

"Sally, can you fix a picnic basket? Dr. Ramsey has agreed that I can take Miss Marrow on a picnic," Steven said glibly.

"Sure, Mr. Steven. That'll do that little angel good. She needs some fresh air and . . . your company, maybe." Sally smiled at him with a knowing look.

 Steven reached out and patted Sally on the shoulder in agreement and said, "I hope so."

Sally went off humming to herself, thinking it would be good to see Mr. Steven and that little angel together. *They would make a good couple.* She busied herself frying chicken for the basket and taking potato salad from the fridge. She placed it into insulated containers to keep it just the right temperature. She had made rolls this morning and, after baking them a golden brown, she wrapped them to keep them nice and warm. A fresh fruit cup would be nice for a picnic to go along with the muffins she had made out of the fresh strawberries she had bought at the market. She made this basket the prettiest one she had ever seen and had it waiting when Steven came into the kitchen.

"Sally, you outdid yourself on that basket!" Steven exclaimed as he picked it up to admire it. It was a wedgewood blue basket with mauve silk flowers around the top. A big bow was tied at the point where the handle was attached. A mauve and blue floral tablecloth showed around the top of the basket and sticking out of the lid. Steven had a backpack with a quilt packed neatly inside it, and he bounded up the stairs to get Annie.

"Are you ready?" Steven asked as he rushed into the suite.

Annie came from the bedroom, dressed in navy slacks with a red sweater. Her blonde hair was tied with a bright red bow and her eyes glowed with excitement. Steven's breath caught in his throat at the sight of her, and he found himself smiling.

"Let's go," he said, finally catching hold of her hand and drawing her to the door.

They entered the kitchen, and Sally beamed with pride as they both complimented her on the basket. Steven picked up the basket as he threw the backpack over his shoulder. Pushing the door open, they both stepped out into the fresh, cool morning air.

Annie looked around as if getting acquainted again with the outdoors. Everything looked as if it had been washed with the morning dew. There was a smell of fall in the air, and the cool breeze caught her blonde curls blowing them across Steven's face.

He could smell the clean apricot fragrance of her hair, as he brushed it aside so he could see where he was going.

Still holding her hand he made for a grassy spot below the huge oak that Annie could see from her window. How often the thought had been in her mind to come here for awhile. Now she was realizing that dream come true and, to make it even better, with someone special.

Steven set the basket beside the tree and the backpack next to it, not turning loose of Annie's hand. No words had been spoken between them up to this moment. They were basking in the beauty of the morning. They began to walk along the stream, watching the ducks that were left swimming lazily along.

"Annie, Jason told me you talked to Ramsey last night," Steven said breaking the silence. "How did that go?"

"He told me he would release me soon," Annie replied. "He also said that what he had intended to accomplish by abducting me was to keep my father's project from being built by distracting him through my disappearance but that he had failed to stop the pregnancy center and adoption home from being under construction," Annie shared.

Steven lowered his head and looked at the ground while he confessed, "I had made up my mind that I was going to talk with him today about your release and tell him I was washing my hands of the whole affair and that I was going to do everything possible to take you home, but . . . ." Steven, finding himself in too deep, let his voice trail off. *How could he tell her that he could not dare to see her leave without spending some time with her? She had made him so angry on Saturday evening, yet he could not bear to think of not seeing her again.*

"Why didn't you, Steven? You must have talked with him about this picnic," she questioned. She was looking at him with a puzzled look on her face. *Was he afraid of an arrest if he pushed for her release and she went home?*

"Let's not talk about it now, Annie. This day is too pretty to spoil with serious talk," Steven said, smiling into her blue eyes.

Annie did not understand his motive. He obviously felt holding her here was wrong, unless, he wanted to prolong facing the authorities. She could think of no other reason he would want to see her held here. She had feared leaving the Manor before she had an opportunity to see him again. She did not want to lose all touch with him. There was something about him that made her heart beat faster, and the pulse in her throat quicken at his touch. They had walked for a long time, and Steven turned back to the direction of the tree. When they reached the tree, he opened the backpack and drew out the quilt. It was a very colorful old quilt -- perhaps it had belonged to someone who lived in the Manor long ago. Annie wondered as he began to unfold it if another couple had used it for a special picnic. *Was this a special picnic to Steven?* She caught hold of two corners of the quilt and helped Steven spread the splash of many colored pieces on the ground.

He dropped down, leaning back against the tree. Then he reached out his hand and caught hers, pulling her down beside him. He continued to hold her hand, causing her pulse to race, and as she looked at him he was smiling as if he knew the effect he was having on her.

"This is just what this doctor ordered," he laughingly said as he looked intently at Annie.

"Your prescription seems good for this patient, Dr. Billups," Annie replied playfully.

"Annie, how was your time with Jason?" Steven had to know.

"We had a good time together. We were both invited to dinner with Dr. Ramsey, you know. Jason spent some time away from the suite, and I spent time reading and thinking about life in general." Annie avoided telling him about Jason's decision as she hoped Jason had already told him.

"Jason seemed unusually happy this morning. I wondered if it had anything to do with the time he spent with you," Steven said, wondering if she would divulge any reason for Jason's change.

"I think any time you have away from your routine helps make you happier. Perhaps time to think helped, too. Life sometimes pressures us into dull thinking, making us unhappy," Annie offered. *Obviously, Jason had not shared his decision with Steven. Time may not have permitted it.*

"What do you do at home that pressures you, Annie? You seem to know what pressure is in a person's life." Steven was thinking about the conversation between Tony Harvey and Nathan Whitten that he had heard at the table next to his in the cafeteria.

"Oh, I don't know. Different things -- school, life in general -- can bring pressures that seem to weigh us down at times. I work part time at temporary jobs, and when I do, I feel pressure enter my life because of additional things claiming the time I want to spend on leisure or hobbies or just being with friends," Annie said thoughtfully, thinking about her friends and the times they had spent together.

Steven saw the opening for his question that was gnawing away at his conscience. Looking at Annie for an answer in ways other than verbal, he ventured to ask a question he wanted an answer for yet feared to know the answer.

"Do you know Dr. Tony Harvey, Annie?" he asked not taking his eyes off hers.

With a look of surprise, Annie blinked and smiled a tiny smile that turned up the corners of her pretty pink mouth. She showed surprise more than anything else, Steven thought.

"Yes, I know Tony," she answered, revealing nothing significant. "I should have thought that you might know Tony as he is also at the Good Samaritan."

"I was in school with him for a time," Steven said. "I had not seen him actually at the Good Samaritan until yesterday when he sat at a table near mine. He introduced me to a friend of his, Nathan Whitten."

"Nathan dates a good friend of mine, Christina Dodson. We have known each other for a long time. I suppose Nathan was the last person with whom I spoke before I was taken." She looked down and began to trace the pattern of the quilt with her free hand.

Steven's mind was at work, to think he was talking with someone who knew her, and he was involved with holding her hostage. *That was a funny way of putting it.* He felt almost like she was holding him hostage. He could think of nothing else when he was away from her, and to think she might leave and he would never see her again brought fear to his heart. *But what about this Tony Harvey? Was she in love with him?*

"Strange, I should meet those two guys at this time," Steven said absently.

"Yes, it is, Steven," she said with a look of sadness in her eyes.

"What about Harvey -- is he serious about anyone?" Steven held his breath for her answer.

"Not that I know about. He and I have gone out a few times. We have enjoyed each other's company, and I think Tony could become serious, but I do not want a commitment of that nature now," Annie said, reflecting in her mind about her dates with Tony. *He was such a nice guy and a fine Christian . . . an ideal person for her, yet . . .*

She caught a smile playing around Steven's eyes and a quirk of his lip. She quickly looked away. She must not let him see her looking for his reaction, and his lips seemed so inviting at times.

Steven felt a wave of triumph. *So Harvey was trying to win her over with this "gem" he had bought for her. Harvey could prove to be an item of competition. Where was his mind taking him, or was that his heart?*

"What do you want out of life, little Annie?" Steven ventured to ask.

"What everyone else wants, I guess. My degree, a happy home and someone to share it with." She was so honest and simple in her answer.

"And what would you look for in choosing that someone to share your life with?" Steven was really getting brave, he thought.

"First of all, he would have to share the same measure of commitment of my faith in God. I suppose, I would prefer him to be even stronger in commitment as he would need to be my spiritual leader. I would want him to love me as I would love him. Not just go through the motions as a lot of couples do, but to be creative in loving each other. Love must be physical as well as spiritual. The only way for true happiness is to be in one accord both spiritually and physically. The emotions of a person are governed by his spiritual life, I believe." Annie was idealistic in her view of love and happiness. She could be called a real romantic by normal standards.

Steven was in deep thoughts by the time she finished. He did not meet any of her standards for someone she would share her life with. *Did he want to? Would Harvey?* Jealousy overtook him at this point.

He wanted to be that person she spent her time with.

"What about you, Steven? What do you want out of life?" she asked, looking at him with interest, a smile playing around her lips. He was still holding her hand, and she felt his grip tighten with her question. *Did this mean anything?* She wondered.

"I want a good practice, I think a private practice in pediatrics. I guess someday I want to settle down. . . . ." He knew he wanted to settle down with her . . . but he had ruined that by being involved with Ramsey. *What else was ruined? She would never see him as this person she described.*

"But you did not tell me what kind of person you wanted to settle down with, Steven," she probed smiling, knowing he was trapped by her question.

"I don't know. I haven't ever been serious about anyone before," he answered, thinking he had gotten out of that.

Annie remembered his words and analyzed them. He had said he had never been serious about anyone . . . . . before. *Did he mean he was serious about someone now? Who?*

"How about lunch? Are you hungry? I hope Sally put a lot in that basket!" He hated to let go of her soft little hand. It felt so good in his big one, like it belonged there.

She pulled her hand away and made preparations to get up. When she did, she lost her balance and would have fallen had Steven not caught her in his arms. Her eyes met his, and neither could look away. Steven held her tighter, yet his arms were so gentle. Annie was afraid he could hear her heart beating. He caught his breath and bent his head dropping a gentle kiss on her sweet pink mouth. Annie closed her eyes and wanted to stay there forever. Steven, afraid he had been too bold, caught her by the shoulders and helped her to stand firmly before reaching for the basket. The magic of the moment passed without any embarrassment.

Annie knelt to help remove the food from the basket. Their hands touched from time to time, and they both knew the excitement of each other's touch. Annie knew she must watch her step with Steven. He had as much as told her he was not a Christian.

They laughed and ate the delicious food which Sally had so lovingly prepared. Then they went for another long walk. They dozed on the quilt in the shade of the big oak and talked about the beauty of the day, but in Steven's mind remained a stolen kiss that was just an appetizer for another one.

A day outside had brought a flush of color to Annie's cheeks and brightness to her blue eyes. She helped Steven fold the quilt and pack it into the backpack and hated to see the day fold into dusk. They had spent most of the afternoon alone on the lawn. Now it was time to return to the suite. How could he lock her in, when she loved her freedom?

They walked hand in hand back to the Manor. Steven saw her beautiful smile and her shiny curls as they blew in the wind.

Just before they reached the patio Annie stopped, turning to Steven, she said, "Thank you, Steven, for a beautiful picnic. I shall never forget this day as long as I live. You have a way of making dark days bright. I am sure you will achieve that goal of yours to be successful in a private practice. I will always think of your kindness when I hear of you." Annie looked at him for a long time.

It was all Steven could do to keep from taking her into his arms and showering her with kisses. She was so sweet and so sincere. Her honesty and openness were almost more than he could bear. He had to see her some more! He could not let her leave here without finding out if he could call on her!

What if he went to jail for his involvement? Her parents would never let him see her again.

CHAPTER TWENTY-THREE

The telephone was ringing incessantly as Julia fumbled with the key in the back door. She had been to the grocery store and left the phone without putting the answering machine on. Andrew had cautioned her about that, as a call could come in from Annie, and they would miss it. Breathless, she lifted the receiver. Thank God, she was not too late.

"Hello," she said, trying to catch her breath.

"Is this the Marrow residence?" a man's voice was asking.

"Yes, it is," Julia answered.

"May I speak with Andrew Marrow?" he requested.

"I am sorry; Andrew is not in at the moment. Could I give him a message?" Julia thought someone might be trying to find out if Andrew was not in and would try to harm her. Their unlisted number discouraged strangers from calling.

"I need to speak with him; is there any way I could reach him at this time?" the man asked.

"Well, yes, you may call him at his office number." She gave Andrew's number.

"Thank you, Mrs. Marrow," the man said politely.

Julia could hear the click as the line was disconnected. *Oh . . . was that something to do with Annie's disappearance?* Almost a week had passed since she had last been seen.

They had tried to keep the faith that God was in control. At times it seemed their faith was weak. Then something would boost them up, and they would gain the victory.

The church had given them much strength. Only this morning, Andrew had felt he must go into the office. Julia had told him if she got discouraged, she would call someone in her Sunday School class to strengthen her. They had spent much of the week in prayer.

Julia busied herself around the house. There was washing,to do, and she went to the utility room to sort the clothes. If she kept busy, she did not imagine the worst. She sorted all the clothes and started the first washer load. Then she picked up her dustcloth to dust the furniture.

The telephone rang. Julia picked it up almost immediately.

It was Andrew. All he said was, "I have some news, I will be home as soon as I can drive there. Annie is fine."

With this he hung up, and Julia began to cry and praise God. Annie is fine, Andrew had said. *How did he know? Did it have anything to do with the first telephone call?*

Andrew was driving into the garage, and Julia ran to meet him. He greeted her with his customary kiss and he was smiling. Taking off his sport coat, he poured a cup of coffee for each of them and pulled out a chair at the kitchen table for Julia.

They were speechless for all this time. Julia could hardly wait to hear what Andrew had learned. It seemed an eternity before he began to tell her his news.

"I received a telephone call -- I believe he called here before calling the office, and you gave him my number. He said to tell you he felt he needed to talk with me, man to man," Andrew began. Julia sat motionless until she nodded her head in agreement.

"He told me he wanted to come over and talk with me face to face about his involvement in this situation, but he would be working until seven in the morning, and he could not rest until we knew that our daughter was all right." Andrew sat for a minute, stirring his coffee. His eyes were filling with tears.

"He sounded like such a fine young man, Julia. I believe he has gotten into this thing without giving it much thought. He is coming by just after seven in the morning to explain the whole thing. Just knowing Annie is safe is a relief, although God has been her protector," Andrew said.

"But who is this man?" Julia questioned.

"He asked me to trust him, that he could not give his name at the phone he was calling from, and assured me that he knew what he was talking about. He also told me that he was with Annie until this morning and that he was prepared to take any punishment that was coming his way." Andrew was speaking intently.

"I thought he sounded so polite over the phone," Julia said trying to sound encouraging.

"I think I better go down to the station and ask Gregory to stop the investigation. I will tell him we have heard from Annie, and she is in no danger. I am convinced it has something to do with the abortion issue. When I asked the young man who called this question, he just said, yes. He could not talk anymore about that from where he was calling. I appreciate his bravery in coming forth with the information he has. It has given us hope and a calmness. I trusted him, and I am looking forward to meeting him in the morning," Andrew said in sincere forgiveness.

"Call the pastor, but ask him to keep it quiet until we hear further, Julia. I won't be long at the police station."

With this Andrew left Julia.

Julia was stunned but happy. Annie was safe and fine. She dialed the pastor's number and delivered the message. He also was thankful to hear of Annie's safety. He and Lori had been so wonderful throughout all of this ordeal. It was a blessing to have Christian friends at a time like this.

Julia had a new lease on life. She began to tidy up the kitchen while her thoughts went to Annie. *Where was she, and what kind of treatment had she received? The young man had said she was fine. He would possibly tell them all about it when tomorrow came. When would they see Annie?* She wondered.

Julia mixed homemade rolls while she waited for Andrew's return. She would take part of the dough and make cinnamon rolls for breakfast. The young man might like to eat breakfast with them. She smiled at the thought.

CHAPTER TWENTY-FOUR

Steven had taken Annie back to the suite, and Annie noticed his hesitancy to go. He had not said anything, just lingered in the sitting room as if he had something on his mind that he could not bring himself to share. She thought how handsome he had looked in his navy sweater and jeans. His trim body complimented the slim-legged jeans, and the wind had rumpled his dark hair that curled at just the right places. He kept it cut so that it would not be hard to manage, she thought.

Abruptly, Steven turned, and opening the door he left without a word. Annie was slightly disap- pointed. She had enjoyed the day so much, and he had given her reason to believe he felt the same. *What was troubling him so now?*

Annie walked to the window and looked out on the back lawn where she and Steven had picnicked just a short time ago. The lone oak tree looked desolate. The sun was casting a golden glow on the dark trunk of the tree and forming silhouettes on the lawn. Soon the lawn would be dark, and the beautiful day would come to a close. It had been one she would never forget, one she would not want to completely forget.

She could feel Steven's arms around her as he caught her just before she would have fallen. She remembered the smell of his aftershave -- so fresh and clean, the softness of his sweater as her cheek brushed against it. But the tenderness and sweetness of his lips on hers was something that s he would cherish. It seemed so natural for him to kiss her. She had never been kissed by many men.

She had let Tony kiss her on one of their dates, but nothing exciting had happened to her. With Steven it was different. Even thinking about it made her pulse accelerate and cause a flutter in her chest. Had he been affected in any way? She wondered.

Tears filled her eyes as she thought about him leaving without saying anything. *Was he sick of her presence?* She knew from the first that he was dangerous. *What had Louis said about him? That he was a charmer of women.* She could understand that now.

Shaking herself, she remembered that Steven was not a Christian, or at least he did not give any evidence that he was one. She knew she must put him out of her mind, and she must put her mind to going home.

Annie decided a nice leisurely bath would help her to relax and take her mind off Steven. She entered the bathroom with anticipation of getting ready for the evening. She decided to bathe, then put her robe on and lie down and rest for a few minutes. The outing had taken a lot out of her, and she would read awhile. Letting the warm water fill the tub, she poured in the bath salts; their fragrance was filling the room -- a nice apricot scent.

She smiled at all the trouble Dr. Ramsey had gone to in order to make her stay here comfortable. How he had thought her father would abandon his service to God, she would never know. Then she remembered Dr. Ramsey was unsaved and did not know one's devotion to God even in times of distress. She stepped into the tub of billowing suds and leaned back for a soak. This was so soothing, she thought. After some time she dried herself off and began to dress.

She would wait until she knew her plans for dinner before she put her outer garments on. Pulling her robe around her, she went into the bedroom and tossed the pillows aside. She picked up the big black Bible that Steven had brought her from the library and lay down on the bed and began to read from God's Word.

After reading she began to pray, "Dear Father, I don't know what is happening to me. I love being with Steven. I know your Word says we are not to be yoked with unbelievers. I do want to be pleasing to You. Please save Steven not just for my sake, but because I know You want to see him give his heart to You. Help me, Father."

Annie fell asleep and was unaware how long she had slept. It was such a restful sleep. By the time she aroused from her nap, darkness had fallen. She went into the sitting room. Rubbing her eyes and going to the door, she found it unlocked. Then she remembered when Steven left she had no recollection of hearing the familiar sound of the lock turning. She stepped into the corridor; she could hear voices, loud and clear. *Were they coming from the library?*

"Dr. Ramsey, I am through. I refuse to be a part of this scheme any longer! I don't know what I was thinking to have ever agreed to involve myself in such a ridiculous plan." It was Steven's voice she heard, and she could hear him pacing.

"But you did involve yourself. I am going to release her soon. I told you that this morning. What has caused you to get so anxious for her release?" Dr. Ramsey sounded angry. Annie wondered what had been said before she heard the conversation.

"I have realized that a lot of things I have, in my stupidity, let myself believe were acceptable, are not. I refuse to lock her in that suite any more! You have seen that your plan has failed. Admit it and let her get on with her life!" Steven's voice held a note of authority.

"How was I to know her father would let nothing interfere with his plans for the center? A loving father would be so preoccupied and frustrated over his only daughter's disappearance that he would forget all else. This man must have a heart of stone." Dr. Ramsey pounded his fist on his desk in his bewilderment.

"No, he has his heart trusting in his God. The same God that Ann . . . Miss Marrow has her trust in. Why do you suppose she has not tried to escape or for that matter torn that suite to shreds? Most girls held against their will would have destroyed the place in anger. But not her. She has trusted God and learned to be content in a situation she could not change." Steven defended Annie and her father. This brought a smile to Annie's face. Although Steven did not seemingly understand completely, he was beginning to see some things that were intriguing to him.

"I suppose you are right about that. I have known girls who would have broken the furniture and windows and . . . . yes, you are right. I have been so caught up in this fight, that I have almost forgotten my real purpose in becoming a doctor. Invite her down for dinner, Dr. Billups. Sally is preparing a good one. We will discuss her going home." With a defeated note in his voice, Dr. Ramsey said no more.

Annie slipped quietly into the suite pulling the door to with as little noise as possible. She went into the bedroom and closed the door. Steven would be up soon, she felt, with the news of dinner. She looked into the closet for the best dress to wear. She chose an ice-blue chiffon with seed pearls around the soft sweetheart neck. The skirt was full and billowy. She then knelt down beside the bed and poured her heart out to God. She knew she needed all the strength possible to be a good witness to Dr. Ramsey and Steven as well.

A knock sounded at the door. Annie, still in her robe, went into the sitting room, and going to the door she opened it to find Steven. He seemed a little nervous but managed a smile that warmed Annie's heart.

"We are invited to dinner. Can you be ready in about thirty minutes?" Steven asked. "It seems Sally is preparing something very special."

"Of course, I'll be ready," Annie said with a smile playing on her lips.

"I'll go get ready. See you in a little while." With this Steven left, closing the door behind him.

Annie could hardly wait to get all dressed for the occasion. This was her last night to be here. She must be alert to any opportunities that she might have to be a testimony of God to these two men. She took special pains to get her makeup just right and brushed her hair until it shown like pulled taffy.

She found a tiny strand of seed pearls in the jewelry case and earrings to match. This was perfect to complete her ensemble.

Her thoughts began to wander. This very possibly could be the last time she would ever be in Steven's presence. The very idea brought tears to her eyes. She must not think of that. *Had her faith in God had any effect on him?*

She was sitting on the sofa when Steven knocked and stuck his head into the room. Annie stood up, and she could not help but see the way Steven looked at her. Her pulse was beating rapidly, and she felt as if she were in a dream world. He was dressed in a dark suit with a light blue shirt and navy and light blue tie. His eyes were as blue as his shirt, and she thought he had the most handsome face she had ever seen.

"Shall we go down?" he asked almost shyly.

Annie did not answer but made a step toward him. As she did he reached for her hand. Annie felt her heart would stop as his hand enfolded hers and they stepped into the corridor.

They descended the stairs, and Annie could see the table looked even more beautiful than it had the night before. Sally had really gone all out. Perhaps she also knew this evening was special, Annie thought. A smile of pleasure was causing her face to glow as Dr. Ramsey came out of the library. He looked quite distinguished himself, thought Annie. He probably was a good doctor who had been taken in by this issue of abortion. She wanted to believe that anyway.

The table was elegant. The snow-white lace cloth was adorned with the most exquisite china. Delicate blue flowers were embossed on gleaming white china. In the center of the table was a long arrangement of mixed flowers. Annie wondered if each evening there were new flowers on the table. It had seemed so each time she had seen it.

Sally began to serve after Dr. Ramsey had seated them. The same seating arrangement as last night except there was Steven instead of Jason. Annie raised her eyes to meet those of Steven across the table. It was hard to look away. She noted a look of anticipation in his deep blue eyes. The light from the candles was flickering, casting shadows and causing strange lights in his glance.

"I do hope your dinner will be pleasant, Miss Marrow," Dr. Ramsey was saying, calling Annie's attention back to himself.

He looked rather handsome, Annie thought. He could be a charming man. She felt a little sorry for him. He was a very wealthy and successful doctor, yet there was a note of sadness about him. She knew the real reason, but how could he be convinced of that?

"I am sure it will be, Dr. Ramsey." She was smiling into his dark eyes.

The appetizer was lobster bisque, and Sally gave Annie a smile as she served her. Annie would hate to leave Sally; she had thought about trying to get in touch with her after she left the Manor. They had developed a special friendship based on their faith in God. Sally had been an encouragement to her while she was here.

"Mmmm . . . . . ," Annie said. "This is delicious."

Steven had been very quiet, she thought. She glanced at him under her long dark lashes. Their eyes met for second, then both looked away.

It appeared to Annie that Dr. Ramsey was having a hard time making conversation, so while they were being served the rest of the meal there was a silence. The cornish hens were baked to a golden brown and served with buttered french peas and onions. The tiny onions looked like over-sized pearls floating in the buttery sauce. Cranberry sauce cut in a flower design completed the look and the taste. Annie thought about the time Sally had spent in preparation for this meal. She must remember to thank her for her effort.

"I understand you went on a picnic," Dr. Ramsey said, looking at the girl. *My, she was pretty tonight! When he had made these plans, he did not know what a lovely daughter Andrew Marrow had.*

Annie's cheeks blushed to a delicate pink shade as she looked up and found Steven's eyes on her. She wondered if he was thinking about the same thing that she was. He was smiling, and she felt herself coloring darkly to the roots of her blonde curls.

"Yes," she said. "Thank you for allowing me to enjoy the beautiful fall day. It would have been a shame to have wasted all that sunshine." She tried to turn the conversation to a light subject.

"You will have to give Dr. Billups credit for prescribing that for you, Miss Marrow," Dr. Ramsey said nodding his head toward Steven. "He was quite persuasive this morning."

Coffee was served by Rosena, and Sally came into the dining room with their dessert. It looked delicious.

"Pistachio cream cake," Sally told Dr. Ramsey after he had looked at it and asked her about it. The cake layers were thin and filled with chocolate chips. It was stacked with pale green frosting and decorated with crushed pistachio nuts and chocolate curls.

"This is very good, Sally," Steven commented.

"Thank you, Mr. Steven," she said before leaving the dining room.

Dr. Ramsey finished his dessert and refilled his coffee cup before he made his announcement to Annie.

"I am going to allow you to return to your home tomorrow, Miss Marrow. I have given it much thought today, and I feel the time has come to release you," he said without looking at her.

Annie looked across the table at Steven. He was smiling, and their eyes met. Annie thought she saw a note of sadness in his eyes before he turned them to Dr. Ramsey.

"Thank you," was all Annie could think of to say. She wanted to say more but could think of no way to get into the subject.

"I am not sure what time you will be able to leave. There are some loose ends I must tie up before you leave. I have thought about the repercussions that all this could cause all of us," he commented with defeat in his voice.

Annie felt uncomfortable, yet she did not answer. She thought he was a smart man, who had not counted the cost involved before his action.

"Steven, are you due at the Good Samaritan first thing in the morning?" he asked looking at Steven.

"Yes, I was allowed to leave today upon your request," Steven answered fearing the consequences of all this involvement.

Steven had been rather quiet during the entire meal. Annie noticed this. What was he thinking? Was he afraid of what all this was going to do to his career?

"Your influence around the Samaritan must be an honored one," Annie said to Dr. Ramsey.

"I suppose so," Ramsey answered almost absently, letting his voice drop as he looked at the cup he held in his hand.

The telephone rang in the foyer, and Sally came to answer. It was for Dr. Ramsey. He returned to the dining room to tell them that he had been called back to the hospital to a very sick patient. This left Steven and Annie alone.

"Would you like to go for a walk out on the deck?" Steven asked.

"That would be nice. I will need a sleeve. I'm sure the temperature has dropped since this afternoon," she answered.

"We will get one," Steven said coming around the table to pull her chair out and escort her to the suite.

The air was crisp and cold. There was no wind, so the light-weight cotton sweater was perfect. Steven and Annie walked on the deck and looked across at the moon as it was rising, casting its reflection on the water of the stream. A stream of golden beads, Annie thought. *How beautiful this place was, the owner must love it here.* She had loved it even though she was a hostage. Now she would be returning home.

Nothing would ever be the same for her, she realized. She had grown up in these few days. She had learned a lot from this traumatic experience. And she would never see Steven again. That thought caused her much sadness. She looked away from the beauty of the stream into the darkness of the night. This was what she would experience . . . from beauty to darkness.

"Annie, I know I have no right to even think about this, but I do hope you can find it in your heart to forgive me for my part in this situation," Steven said without hope.

"There is nothing to forgive on your part, Steven. You have shown me only pleasant times while I have been here. I will treasure them as an oasis in a desert," she said in her sweet way.

"I have been stupid to even be involved in this kind of thing. I wanted the approval of someone with Ramsey's prestige. I felt I needed it. Now I'm not so sure," he said.

"Steven, that is something you will have to deal with and settle in your own mind and heart. I remember you saying you needed his help in your career. He seems a well thought of man in some areas. His involvement in the abortion issue is only part of his career as a physician. Until you and he realize where you stand there, I guess your need will remain," Annie said, trying to draw Steven into discussing his beliefs.

"Annie, let's not talk about that subject tonight," Steven said.

Annie felt that might be a good idea. She had given him enough to think about previously.

Steven took hold of her hand and began to walk down to the big oak. The lawn was soft from the dew that had fallen, and it became hard for Annie to walk in her heels. He slipped his arm around her waist to steady her. She knew this was not the thing she should allow, knowing the way he affected her, but somehow she could not pull away. Her heart pounded in her chest at his touch.

At the oak he stopped, and they stood for a long time looking out on the stream decked with diamonds as the moon cast its light on the moving water. Annie shivered from the night air. Steven tightened his hold around her waist; then he suddenly caught her with his other hand and pulled her to him.

She knew in her heart what was going to happen, and knew she should not give in, but his lips found hers in a sweet tenderness. She wanted to stay here forever, but her conviction brought her to pull away. He released her reluctantly. They returned to the house without saying a word. They did not need to. Annie knew she would never forget that kiss, although she could never know the ecstasy of another.

CHAPTER TWENTY-FIVE

The doorbell of the Marrow home rang with determination. Andrew had called the office earlier to tell them he would be late arriving today and left some letters on his computer for his secretary. He and Julia anxiously waited in the kitchen for their visitor. Julia had baked the cinnamon rolls and had them iced. They had been up since five o'clock as neither could sleep.

Andrew opened the door to find a tall good-looking dark-haired, brown-eyed young man standing there. He seemed a little uncomfortable, and his eyes could not meet those of Andrew.

"I am Jason Putzer. I called you yesterday to give you news of your daughter. May I come in?" he asked.

"Please do. Julia and I are having a cup of coffee in the kitchen," Andrew replied. "Would you have some with us?"

This man seems unusually calm, thought Jason. He was the most trusting person he had ever seen. *No wonder his daughter had such strength.*

"Julia," Andrew said, "this is Jason Putzer. He has news of Annie." Julia came forward and shook hands with Jason as Andrew pulled out a chair for him at the side of the table. The sun came in the window beaming its rays on the black hair of this young man.

"Sir, I will first of all set your mind at rest about your daughter. She is well cared for and is perfectly safe. I will not divulge her whereabouts, if that is permissible, as I am breaking a trust, so to speak, just being here. I could not bear to let another day go by without coming to you and asking your forgiveness for my part in the situation. I know you could put me behind bars for the kidnapping of your daughter, if you choose to do so. You see, I was the one who picked her up," Jason lowered his head. He could not look these two trusting people in the face after causing them such grief.

"I don't understand, Mr. Putzer," Andrew said bewildered as to how this man was able to persuade Annie to go with him without a scuffle.

Jason told the story, leaving out the other members involved. He felt every man had to account for himself. All he knew was that he could not live another day with this on his conscience.

The parents sat with their eyes riveted on him until he finished telling them about his deceit and then about his spending time with Annie.

"I just want you to know, Mr. Marrow, you have a daughter to be proud of," Jason said, finally able to meet their eyes.

"Mr. Putzer, ... " Andrew began.

"Please call me Jason, Mr. Marrow," Jason interrupted.

"Jason, I think you are a very conscientious young man, and a courageous one also. To think that you admit to abducting Annie and guarding her, as you say, and then you cared enough to call us and let us know of her safety tells me you are to be trusted."

Andrew put his hand on the stooped shoulder of the tall young man.

"Thank you for coming to us," Julia said.

Jason heard the voice of her daughter who always was so thankful for every little thing. He remembered her even thanking Dr. Ramsey.

"I want to tell you something else. Because of your daughter I am a changed person. I had a dear grandmother who wanted me to commit my life to Christ. The influence of Annie has caused the Holy Spirit to prompt my heart into making that commitment. Sunday night after I left the suite where Annie was being kept, I picked this up."

At this point he reached into his inside coat pocket and brought out the folded piece of note paper. "Annie had given this to me before I had left her room and I had stuffed it into my pocket to read later. On going to bed I opened it up and began to read. My heart was touched, and I knelt and surrendered my life to Christ." Jason finished with tears filling his eyes.

He handed the paper to Julia. She recognized the handwriting, and tears streamed down her cheeks. She came around the table and hugged the young man.

"I thank God for a loving grandmother, Jason," she said. "And for using our Annie to remind you of your upbringing."

"Let us thank God right now for what has come of this traumatic situation. He is so good to us. He has brought glory to Himself through a dark hour." Andrew said and bowed his head and reached for Jason's hand and the hand of Julia.

They thanked God for all He had done.

After the prayer they sat silently for a few moments. Then Andrew said to Julia, "Honey, I'll bet our new son would like some cinnamon rolls. You don't mind us calling you our son, Jason, do you? We have many sons and like having another."

"That is what Annie said when I told her of my decision. She said we were now brother and sister. I can't think of a nicer sister to have than Annie." Admiration shined in Jason's eyes.

CHAPTER TWENTY-SIX

The morning had dawned sunny and mild. Annie had not slept well and was up early in anticipation of going home. She had showered and dressed in the grey skirt and pink sweater she had worn on her arrival at the Manor. She took one look at herself in the mirror and realized she looked a little tired, so she spent extra care to apply her makeup to cover any tell-tale signs of her sleepless night. She looked around the bedroom and thought how long it had seemed since she was in her own bed even though it had only been a few nights.

So much had happened since her birthday. Ironic, how much older she felt than when she came here. *Was that maturity?* She smiled to herself thinking about Christina and Katie and their eagerness to hear all about her stay here. She thrilled at the thought of surprising her parents with her return, although she knew they were trusting God with her absence.

Sally came into the sitting room and called to her. Annie had enjoyed the companionship of Sally. Each day they had spent time talking, and Sally had been a great friend to her. When Sally had come to clean the suite Annie helped her in spite of Sally's objections.

"Good morning, Sally," Annie said with a smile. "You are here early this morning. I thought I would be the only one rambling around at this time of day. You know Dr. Ramsey has promised I could go home today."

"Yes, angel, I'm glad this mess is about over. But you know how much I'm going to miss you," Sally said with mixed emotions.

"And I'm going to miss you, Sally. You have been wonderful to me, and I shall never forget you and all the kind things you have done. Do you stay at the Manor most of the time?" Annie asked.

"Yes, honey, Sam and I live here year round. He is the gardener, you know, and we have a little suite downstairs all our own." Sally beamed with pride.

"I will come back to see you, Sally. I promise. It may take some time to get back, but I promise, if God wills, I will come and visit you," Annie said, hugging the little woman to her.

Sally and Annie tidied the suite, and Sally insisted Annie go down to the kitchen with her to enjoy her breakfast. Annie agreed, and they sat in the little nook with the morning sun streaming through the bay window on Annie's blonde curls.

This breakfast was a special one that Sally had prepared for Annie. She had made butterscotch pecan rolls served with bacon and eggs. The coffee was Swiss mocha, and Annie felt like a princess as Sally fussed around her. She exclaimed each time Sally would bring another serving for her to eat.

"Sally, you are going to make me fat, with all your good food. Thank you for preparing something special for me today," Annie said with all sincerity.

Annie returned to the suite for a quiet time before leaving the Manor. This had truly been an unusual experience in her life. She picked up the big black Bible. Sally had promised to return it to the library after Annie had left. That Book had given much strength to Annie during her stay here. Steven had been so sweet to bring it up to her.

Where was Steven, she wondered. She did not see anything of him or Dr. Ramsey when she was eating breakfast. They must have already left the Manor for the hospital.

A touch of sadness gripped her heart as she thought of Steven. *Would she ever see him again?* He had been so quiet last night when they returned to the suite. He had left her at the door, squeezing her hand before he turned to go back down the stairs. He had not even said goodbye. She had been speechless, as well. *Should she have said more? What could she say?*

Tears filled her eyes, and she began to blink them away. She knew she could not see him, even if he wanted to, because she was much too serious about her feelings for him as it was, and she had never dated an unsaved man in her life before. She had been taught that there was a danger of coming to love someone that one dated, and this was the reason she could not see Steven even if he called her. He was probably glad it was soon to be over.

Annie walked to the window which had played such a big part in her life since coming to this suite with Jason. This window was her picture of the world outside. It had brought sunshine into her life on the days when the sun was out, and it had washed the world on the days of rain.

She looked across the lawn where she and Steven had walked yesterday on their picnic and again last night when they strolled down to the big oak. That old tree shared her secret, towering above her and Steven when he had held her close and kissed her with such tenderness. She could almost feel his lips on hers now. The sweetness of that moment would be part of her for the rest of her life. *Would she be able to go on with life back home as if nothing had ever happened?*

She heard a knock at the door, and turning around she saw none other than Dr. Ramsey, himself. She had thought maybe Jason would take her home. But Dr. Ramsey was asking her if she was ready to go.

Picking up her purse, the only thing she had brought with her, and the little notebook, with the little note from Steven still in it, she walked to the door.

"Did Sally pack your clothes, Miss Marrow?" he asked.

"This is all I have, Dr. Ramsey. I could not think of taking all those expensive things you provided while I was here," Annie said calmly.

"I intended you to have them. They were bought for you, and much care was taken that they fit and be the colors that were becoming to you," he said.

"I have been curious about the clothes. How did you know my size and taste so well?" Annie ventured.

"Computer age, Miss Marrow. Several months ago you and two of your friends entered a drawing at one of the smart shops where your size, color preference, style, etc. was registered. A receptionist who was also working for me at the time worked on weekends at the shop. Does that explain?"

Annie remembered the day well. Christina and Katie were with her. She remembered the fun they had, unaware of it being used in a negative way.

"I am sorry, maybe there will be someone else who will fit my build and color combination," Annie said. "They are lovely. Most any girl would love them," she added with a little sadness to leave them, yet she did not dare take them.

"Very well," he said.

Annie walked through the door with her head down. She was glad this was almost over, and yet there had been some pleasant memories she was leaving behind. No, she was not leaving them -- they would be with her the rest of her life.

When they were well on their way down the long winding drive through the trees before reaching the main road, Annie spoke to Ramsey.

"I'm surprised that you are taking me home yourself. I assumed Jason would do it for you," she said matter-of-factly.

"You did not think I had the courage to face up to my deeds, did you, Miss Marrow?" He looked at her with a quizzical look on his face.

"I suppose you are right," she said in return.

"I am afraid I have given you a bad impression of myself through what I have done," he said keeping his eyes on the road.

"Well, I'm trying to believe the best, but I admit I am a bit puzzled by your actions. You have a fine reputation as a doctor, and I have come to the conclusion that you found yourself caught up in this abortion issue for some reason, and in the heat of it all you did not think through your plans thoroughly before you acted in my case," Annie offered.

"I think too much is made by you people concerning abortion in the first place, causing a big disturbance from both sides," he said not wanting to face making a decision.

"That would be a reasonable way of thinking for you, Dr. Ramsey," Annie said with boldness.

"Why do you say that?" he asked.

"Obviously you do not believe the Bible to be a guide for your life," was all she said as she looked out the side window at the countryside they were passing.

"Let us say I do not place the same emphasis on it that you seem to," Dr. Ramsey replied.

"That is a pity as the Author of the Book is the Creator of the bodies you are responsible for restoring to good health; as well as those you are destroying," Annie commented.

The rest of the way to Annie's home was a quiet ride. Neither of them spoke. Annie was thinking about their arrival. Would her father be there? Would Dr. Ramsey drop her off or would he go in to meet her family? She glanced at the man behind the wheel -- he sat with a solemn look on his face. *Had he a plan to free himself of what he had done?*

The big Park Avenue rounded the corner on the street where Annie lived. Her heart beat faster as she thought about seeing her parents again. Ramsey turned into her drive, and the car came to a halt. Dr. Ramsey jumped out and came around to open her door. Annie saw that her father's car was still home.

Walking up to the front door, Annie was thinking about how Ramsey would approach her father. She reached into her bag for the key to the lock. Ramsey took it from her, as any gentleman would, and unlocked the door.

Annie opened the door calling, "Mom! Dad!" She waited for an answer.

Immediately her parents hurried into the foyer, and Julia caught Annie in her arms. Andrew smiled at the man behind her. Reaching out his hand, he introduced himself.

"I am Andrew Marrow. Dr. Jake Ramsey, I believe."

"Hello," was all Ramsey could say, extending his hand reluctantly, fearing the worst.

Ramsey looked at Annie and Julia standing side by side.

"This is my wife, Julia, ... Dr. Ramsey," Andrew said.

There were some awkward moments before Dr. Ramsey turned to Andrew and said, "Could I speak with you alone, sir?"

"Of course," Andrew replied. "Excuse us, girls," he said to Julia and Annie and led Dr. Ramsey into his study to the right of the foyer entrance. The men closed the door, and Julia and Annie went into the kitchen.

"Oh, Annie, we were so worried about you, honey," Julia cried.

"I know, Mom. I wished you could know that I was safe but could think of no way to get the word to you. I have been given the best of care, just taken out of the picture to try to deter Father's progress with the center. I am so thankful that he was able to go ahead with the building before the permit expired. That was the purpose of the whole plan. Dr. Ramsey thought Daddy would be so upset and disturbed that he would think of nothing else and let the permit slip and delay or even halt altogether the building of the center. Then the property would revert back to the original heirs, and the Good Shepherd Home for Women would become only a dream of the past," Annie explained.

The police thought it might have something to do with the abortion issue," Julia said. "They were at a loss on leads to your disappearance though."

"I must tell you about that. It was partly my fault for playing into Ramsey's hands. The guy that picked me up, I mistook for Daddy's new assistant, Kip Thornton, and when he told me Daddy wanted me to meet him for lunch, I went willingly without fear." Annie shook her head as though disgusted with herself.

"I know, dear. We have heard all about that part of it," Julia said with a smile.

Annie looked at her mother with bewilderment. *How could she know? Who told her?*

Then finding her voice, she asked, "But who told you?"

"Jason came to see us this morning early after calling your father yesterday and assuring us of your safety." Julia was smiling at her daughter, thanking God for her.

Annie smiled with tears in her eyes. *Dear Jason. He was so kind and good. What courage it took to face her parents after what he had done. When he got his heart right he had set out to make restitution for his wrongs.* Thank you, God, for Jason, Annie prayed.

Julia poured Annie a cup of coffee, and they sat at the table talking about the whole experience. Julia confessed about the surprise party and the wonderful ways all Annie's friends had been such a comfort to them throughout this time.

Annie shared her experiences, or part of them. Julia could see a difference in Annie. She had matured; she had learned a lot about faith in action. This was thrilling to Julia and frightening at the same time. Annie was no longer her little girl; she was a young woman, able to stand on her own with God.

"I just want to go upstairs and see my room. I want to call Christina and Katie as soon as they get in from school. I do hope I can make up all my work I missed at school without a lot of difficulty. Perhaps Daddy can go with me to see the Dean of Students tomorrow so that he can help me verify my story. I don't think I can go today. I have to give some thought to what I need to do. I love you, Mother," Annie said, hugging her mother before going up the stairs.

CHAPTER TWENTY-SEVEN

The drive back to the hospital gave Steven time to organize his thoughts. He was unaware of the beauty of the morning sun gleaming on the new day. He was thinking about a girl, an unusual girl with big blue eyes and blonde curls that were a temptation to muss up. He smiled as he thought about her smile, a smile that could melt the ice around even Ramsey's heart. *What was the trip like back to Annie's home? What did those two find to talk about?* Steven was almost jealous of the time Ramsey had to spend with her this morning.

Steven's thoughts went to his waking up. After he had dressed, he had walked to the door of the suite and had wanted to go in and say goodbye to her, but somehow he could not find the courage to do so. *He would forget her in a few days. Out of sight, out of mind, was that not the way the old saying went?*

Shaking himself, he brought his attention back to his driving. The hospital was ahead, and he would miss his exit off I-81 if he was not careful.

Upon arrival at the hospital, he was thrown into the routine of the usual day. There seemed to be an unusual number of sick children of all ages. His workload was extremely heavy, which he kept telling himself was good therapy. *What should he do about contacting Annie? Should he try? What would happen about his involvement in this case? Was he ready to get it behind him, whatever the outcome?*

Steven entered the cafeteria later than usual today. He spotted Tony Harvey and Nathan Whitten. They called to him to join them. Why not, he asked himself. They had enjoyed talking on a couple of occasions. Now that he knew how Annie felt about Tony, he could handle it. They would have no reason to know he even knew her.

Picking up his sandwich and iced tea, he made his way to their table. Nathan was the first to speak.

"I have heard your page quite frequently today, Dr. Billups," Nathan said smiling.

"Please call me Steven. Every child around Tug Hill Plateau must be at the Good Samaritan. We have some very ill little ones," Steven said as he placed his tray on the table.

"We have been rather busy on our floor, also," Tony offered.

"What has been going on with you guys?" Steven asked, hoping to hear some interesting news.

"Nothing out of the ordinary," Nathan replied.

"Oh, by the way, Nathan, have you spoken to Christina this morning?" Tony asked.

"Not since before she left for class. I'll call her after three. We have a date to go to a concert of some sort at the college tonight. Why?" Nathan was curious.

"I received a call from Mrs. Marrow during one of the surgeries I was observing this morning, and she asked me to call her around two o'clock. I can't imagine what she wants. I wondered if you had heard anything."

They did not reveal anything about Annie, but Steven knew this must have something to do with her return home. He hoped his expression would not reveal anything, but he had to know what was going on somehow. He hated to use the friendship of these great guys for a selfish purpose, but they were his only link with Annie.

"I hope it is good news," Nathan said without further comment, not having any idea that Steven would understand.

"Me, too," was all Tony said.

Steven felt self-conscious being with them under false pretense. How he wished he could honestly be friends with them. They were so sincere and open, and he was wearing a mask of deceit. A smile crept across his face, as a beautiful smiling face with defiance in the eyes came to his mind. That is what she had told him. *If only she knew how firmly that mask was in place now.*

"You seem to be in a world of your own, Steven. Remembering some pleasant date?" Tony questioned looking at him with a sly grin plastered on his face.

"I guess you could call it that. We doctors have so little free time, we have to make the most of every occasion and relive them to the fullest." Steven chuckled to cover up.

"You have that right," Tony said. "It is hard to establish a relationship with someone keeping the hours we do. A girl has to be a very understanding person to even put up with us." Tony laughed, wishing he had an opportunity to know where the one girl he wanted to be with was at the time.

"Well, it's hard for any of us," Nathan said thinking about Christina and how understanding she had been with him having to break a date in order to fulfill some duty at the hospital.

At that moment Steven was being paged and said his goodbyes.

Tony and Nathan promised to call as soon as they could get away for some leisure, perhaps a game of golf.

The rest of the day was hectic and kept Steven's mind from straying to memories he had made with Annie. He thought about Tony and his call from Mrs. Marrow. *What had she wanted to share with him -- that Annie had been returned home?*

Running into Jason in the hall proved to be a bright spot in Steven's day. Jason still had a big smile on his face. He was especially different, Steven thought. He must find time to talk with Jason. It seemed Jason was as busy as he was today. If he could find a minute, he would go down to Therapy and make a dinner date with him, that is, if they could arrange it.

Steven felt cut off from Annie. *Why had he not gone in to say goodbye this morning? Why had he not asked her if he could see her after she went home?* He did not feel worthy to see her after what he had done.

The days passed and spread into weeks with Steven staying at the hospital more and more. He hardly ever went out anymore. He was so tired at night after being on the floor all day, and if he was on duty at night, he slept during the day but did not seem to get rested. On occasion he had gone out to jog.

One day at lunch, Nathan and Tony were waiting for him outside the cafeteria. They had noticed the vast change in him. Where he had always been the life of the party, so to speak, he seemed to have lost his zest for life. They were concerned for their new-found friend.

"Steven, come on over to the far table. You look like you need a break," Tony suggested.

"Is this Dr. Harvey prescribing for me?" asked Steven trying to be cheerful.

"I guess you could say that," Tony said with a laugh.

"He does that for all of us, Steven," joined in Nathan. They were trying to cheer up Steven.

They picked up their order and made for the corner table away from the other diners.

"What's been going on with you, Dr. Billups?" Tony asked. "Are you trying to drown yourself in work?"

He was genuinely concerned for Steven, and Steven could tell by the inflection in his voice.

If only you knew, thought Steven. "I guess I am trying to make up some lost time. I was off for a few days and I felt I could work hard and catch up," Steven offered, disguising his real reason.

"Man, you need to get out more. Why don't you come to a party we are having for a friend of ours on Saturday? You could get off, couldn't you?" Nathan asked. "Tony and I would like you to meet some of our friends; I think you might enjoy them."

Steven was shocked! *Is it possible that they talking about a party for Annie? How would he get out of this without being obvious?* He could not go to that party! He could not just show up with these guys and show how deceitful he really was -- Annie would hate him.

"I will think about it. If I can arrange it, I will." Steven had to find a way to be needed desperately at the hospital. He could not just refuse to go.

The two guys let it go at that telling him they would be praying that he would find a way to go. Then they began to talk about something very interesting to Steven -- Annie.

"There is this girl," Nathan began. "She is a friend of Christina, Tony and me. She was abducted by someone and held hostage for about a week. We are surprising her with this party. She missed her birthday surprise party because she was taken on her birthday."

Steven wished he were anywhere but here. He was the most miserable person in the world. *Did Jason know it was Annie's birthday? How was he going to be able to stand much more of this talk?* Yet he wanted to know more.

Tony was speaking, "She has been home a few weeks and has had time to settle back into the routine of things. She missed a week of classes at JCC, but she talked to the Dean, and she has worked hard to make up her work at school. She is so interested in doing her best. She makes great grades anyway; I know she can handle it." He spoke with authority about her.

"You would like her," Nathan said in all sincerity. "Her parents are the greatest. All her friends enjoy visiting in her home."

All Steven could say was, "I'm sure I would like to meet her." He was subdued with the thought of Annie. Yes, he would love to see her, to hold her. . . Steven was brought back to the present by Nathan's voice.

"Christina is so excited about this party. I think I will have to tie her feet to the floor to keep her on the ground."

"Knowing Christina, I can believe that. She is a great girl, also," Tony said.

"How is your relationship going with Annie?" Nathan ventured to ask.

"It could stand some spark of life. She seems so preoccupied since returning home. Has Christina said anything to you about her talking about what kind of experience she had while she was away?" Tony asked Nathan.

"Christina has also noticed a difference in her. Annie has only told Christina that her time away was pleasant for the most part, that she even enjoyed much of it. Her worry about her parents and friends, the fact of being held against her will, and the initial fear were the worst things she had to deal with. She said when God showed her that she should be content in whatever circumstance she was in, she began to see opportunities to touch the lives of others instead of focusing her thoughts on herself. She shared with Christina that she had met some nice people. Christina doesn't tell me everything. They do a lot of girl-talk," Nathan said and laughed.

Tony laughed and commented, "We probably could not understand that girl-talk anyway."

Steven only listened, contemplating his plight and holding on to every word Nathan had to say. It thrilled him to just hear from her. He could visualize her pretty face. Oh, I must come back to reality, he thought.

"I have taken Annie out to dinner a couple of times. She did tell me that we were good friends, and she wanted me to know she treasured our friendship. That sounded to me like I did not have much chance in the romantic area unless our friendship builds into love. You know I am extremely fond of her. I have even thought I loved her, but I am putting it into God's hands to work out what He sees fit," Tony said.

"Have you given her the gift you bought her?" Nathan asked.

"I tried to," Tony said. "She felt it was too expensive. She asked me to please give her time to know her feelings about it. You know that little necklace is nothing serious, but that is the way Annie is," Tony said without malice.

"Sorry, Steven, old boy, that we got carried away. Hope we did not bore you with our concern for our friend," Tony said apologetically.

"Not at all," Steven said. *If they only knew.* How he hated this mask he was wearing. *What was he going to do?*

"I better get back to the ole Good Samaritan and its business." said Steven. "Thank you guys for inviting me to lunch with you."

With this Steven left the table and strolled with his hands in his pockets toward the swinging door. He was gone.

"You know, Tony, that guy needs to know the Lord, and he is getting to the place where we need to be alert to the right time to share Christ with him," Nathan commented.

"You're right. We will need to pray for him that the Holy Spirit will stir him up and prepare his heart -- like you guys prayed for me." Tony slapped Nathan on the shoulder before tossing his trash into the cafeteria receptacle.

CHAPTER TWENTY-EIGHT

Annie settled into school again, trying hard to catch up. Annie felt sure she could handle the extra work some way. As she drove to school she thought about what a cold morning it was. The temperature had dropped several degrees during the night. It felt good to be on the outside and experience the change in the seasons. Winter was near. It felt good to be driving again.

She smiled to herself thinking about the curiosity of her two dear friends about the days she had spent at the Manor. Christina had remarked several times that Annie seemed different. Annie knew in her heart that Christina was right. Something had happened to her that had changed her while at the Manor.

Besides the fact that she had gained some spiritual insights about her life, she had met someone who had stolen her heart. *Would she ever get over Steven?* The thought of him brought many emotions to surface in her heart.

She turned her thoughts to Tony. She had hated to tell Tony that she could never be serious about him. She did not tell him why. She could not explain that someone else had her love -- someone whom she could never enjoy loving because he did not share her faith. That someone who was not even aware of her love for him. It hurt that he had not called or tried to see her in all these weeks. *Was he afraid of the repercussions of his involvement?* She knew there were many women in his life. *He did not need her.*

Annie was happy that her father had agreed with her that no charges should be made as she was not seriously harmed. Chief Gregory could not comprehend their thinking when her father told him he wanted all indictments dropped, if there had been any against Dr. Ramsey and anyone else involved in the abduction. He had agreed there would be no problem in that area.

Annie smiled as she remembered her father's account of Dr. Ramsey and his conversation on the day Ramsey brought her home -- the shock on Ramsey's face when he was received as a friend instead of a foe. Is that not what the Bible was speaking of, thought Annie, when it said the simple would confound the wise? God's gentle way confounds the people who are given to fighting against one another. How she prayed that Dr. Ramsey would let the truth sink into his heart and follow it.

She thought it was clever and wise of her father to require Ramsey to meet with him once a month for a conference. Dr. Ramsey had agreed, and Andrew had said that their first meeting had gone really well. Annie knew her father would witness Christ to him. She smiled at this. Funny how her father had used this act of Ramsey's to give him an opportunity to share his faith with the doctor. Ramsey could not afford to refuse.

Her thoughts turned to Jason. He had been to the house a couple of times since she had been home. Her parents had grown so fond of him, and he was like that brother she had always wanted. He had been the one to give her news about Steven. He told her he had spoken to Steven on a few occasions, and no mention had been made concerning Annie. He did not think Steven knew about his coming forth with her whereabouts. He had told Steven, the last time they met, about his rededication of his life to Christ.

This had been the first time they had really had any time together alone.

Jason had been in church regularly, when he wasn't working. Annie's gang of friends had invited him to several of their get-togethers, but as yet he had not been able to come. Annie was excited about meeting Christina and Katie for lunch today in the little restaurant near JCC. She was looking forward to being alone with them. Usually Nathan and Tony or some of the other people were around, but today just the three of them could share their innermost thoughts.

Annie's classes went well. She was feeling more comfortable getting back into the swing of things. Amazing what a few days can do for a person!

Walking to the restaurant, Annie pulled her bright red jacket close to her slim body. The wind was blowing her blonde curls topsy-turvy. The warmth of the restaurant felt good. She caught sight of Christina and Katie immediately. They had secured a very private booth near the back of the restaurant. *Good, they could enjoy each other's company in private.*

"Hello, Annie," the two called out at the same instant, then laughed at their chorus.

"Hello, you two," Annie said smiling.

"I am starving," said Katie, who loved to eat even though it appeared she never gained a pound.

"What are we having?" asked Christina looking at the menu with interest.

"How about a nice grilled chicken sandwich?" Annie suggested. "I think that is what I want and fries. I'll have tea."

After the orders were given, the girls settled down to serious talk.

Christina was talking about her date with Nathan. She and Nathan were so suited for each other, thought Annie. Katie was eager to share her latest news about her date, and then they turned to Annie with questioning eyes, eager to hear the news of their friend's budding romance.

"What about you and Tony?" Katie ventured to ask. "We heard about the beautiful sapphire pendant he bought for you."

"Tony is a great guy," Annie commented. "I wish I could care for him in any way other than a friend. We are great friends, but that is as far as it goes. I could not accept such an expensive gift. I did not want to give him any encouragement that there could be anything more than what we have now," Annie admitted and looked down at her plate. *How could she tell her two friends that she could never love anyone?*

Katie and Christina looked at each other over the table. They were shocked and puzzled. Tony and Annie seemed so right for each other. Both were such wonderful Christians, liked the same things and loved people.

Finally Christina, seeing Annie was silent and contemplative, asked, "Is there someone else in your life, Annie?"

"Not really, I have met someone who has made me know I can't get serious about anyone else," Annie confessed without revealing anything more.

There was silence as each girl looked at Annie as though she was a stranger. *What did she mean? Who was this guy, and where had they met? Why was she not seeing him?*

"But, Annie, tell us about him," said Katie with enthusiasm, coming out of her state of speechlessness.

"I don't know if I should. I have been suppressing any thought of him," Annie said with sadness overtaking her. Her blue eyes looked pleadingly at her friends.

"But why ever would you do that?" Katie asked again.

Christina sat looking intently at her friend. She was trying to make some sense out of Annie's statement.

"Well, for one thing, he is not a Christian. I could not get serious about someone who did not share the same faith I do, and then he, with

191

all probability, does not feel the same way about me," Annie finished and her mouth quivered.

This was the first time she had shared her dilemma with anyone. She had wanted to share with her mother but could not find the opportunity to do so. It had seemed so much easier to tell her two close friends, she supposed, because they were near her own age.

"But where did you meet him? At school?" Christina asked without taking her eyes from Annie's face.

Annie looked Christina in the eye and replied, "No, he was at the Manor as one of my guards."

The girls locked eyes and knew they had to hear more. Christina was the first to speak. Their lunch now seemed so unimportant.

"Do you want to tell us about him, and is there any way we can help?" Christina asked.

"There is really nothing much to tell. He was my guard for only a few days. There was something different about him from the first -- he was the handsomest guy I have ever met."

Annie smiled as she remembered looking into Steven's eyes when first they met.

"He and I did a lot of talking, and he found a Bible for me to read, also sent me a notebook as he found out I loved to write each day. One evening he arranged for us to have a fancy dinner in the suite, candlelight and all. Then one day before I was released, he planned a picnic on the back lawn. We spent the day walking along the stream that flowed at the back of the Manor and sat under a big oak tree."

Annie omitted the most precious moments spent, not wanting to share those treasured kisses with anyone, knowing how sacred they seemed between people who loved each other. Well, that was her opinion, she thought.

"That sounds so sweet," Christina said with stars in her eyes. She was such a romantic at heart.

Katie was eager to know more. She felt Annie was holding

something back.

"But how do you know he is not a Christian?" Katie inquired.

"He was brought up going to church, but he showed no signs of knowing Christ in a personal way. I think he was intrigued with some things I shared with him, but he became angry with me when we discussed faith in God in a personal way. That led me to believe that he knew about God, but that is not enough, you know that. I could not allow myself to pursue a relationship that could lead to uniting with an unbeliever. That is, if he was interested, which he's not. He did not even come by the day I left to say good-bye, and I have not heard from him all these weeks." Annie finished with a note of hopelessness in her voice.

They wanted to know much more, but Annie was experiencing so much pain. The two girls hugged their friend, and they all agreed to pray that God would work in this person's life as well as comfort Annie.

After this they talked of school and clothes, and Annie told them about Dr. Ramsey asking her father if he could send Annie all the beautiful things he had bought for her use while at the Manor. At first Andrew refused, and then after the second meeting with Dr. Ramsey, Andrew came home and told Annie she should accept them. He felt they were being obstinate about those good clothes hanging in that closet. Andrew explained that Ramsey looked at the gift of the clothes as a way of making restitution for the harm done.

The girls became eager to see them as Annie described some of her favorite dresses. They laughed, and when they left the restaurant they all felt better.

Their friend was the same Annie, yet she was more mature.

Upon arriving home, Annie was told the clothes had arrived. Julia was ecstatic. These were the most beautiful dresses she had seen. She had agreed with Annie at first that she did not think it would be wise to accept them, but Andrew had assured her that it was best as a kind of restoration process for Dr. Ramsey. She hoped he was right. He usually was.

Annie busied herself hanging them in her closet with Julia there to supervise. They laughed and talked about the expense and trouble Ramsey had gone to in order to achieve his goal, only for God to cause it to fail.

Annie shared with her mother how Ramsey had been able to learn her size, style, and color combinations. They had been praying for the doctor. Andrew had whistled when he saw the loot.

"Annie, you are going to have to find yourself a young man to get serious about to take you to dinner so you can wear all those pretty things. Dr. Ramsey has good taste in clothes," He said and pinched his daughter on the cheek like he had done when she was little.

"Maybe she already has, Andrew," Julia said looking at Annie with question. "She seems awfully quiet these days. We women can sense things you men can never see with your eyes."

Annie looked at her mother and decided it was time she shared her secret with her.

Andrew went down to watch the evening news, and Annie and Julia stayed behind to have a serious mother-daughter talk. Julia agreed to pray for the young man. Annie did not tell her his name or anything about his profession -- just that he was unsaved and that he was the only man she felt she could ever really love.

CHAPTER TWENTY-NINE

The days were getting gradually colder, and snow storms were promised. Things at the hospital were as busy as ever. Jason and Steven had finally found time to get together, and Jason had shared his testimony with Steven. Jason had shown Steven the little piece of paper Annie had written out for him.

Steven had looked at the neatly formed words on the notebook paper and felt a closeness to Annie. How he longed to have the relationship that Jason had as far as being able to visit in her home! Jason had told him about her parents and their openness with him.

Before leaving Steven, Jason had asked if he had not tried to see Annie since she had left the Manor. Steven just shook his head. Jason wondered what had happened between them. He had felt there was a strong attraction between the two while Annie was held hostage. He had prayed for Steven's salvation. He planned to talk with Annie about his friend the next time he saw her. Before leaving Steven he reminded him that they needed to get together more often.

Steven had not seen Tony and Nathan for a couple of days, and Saturday, when the party was to be held, was approaching. *He knew he would have to make sure that he would be forced to work. He just could not go to that party, as desperately as he wanted to go.* As he came out of the elevator, he saw Nathan coming up the corridor.

"Would you like to join us for lunch?" Nathan asked Steven.

Steven knew he wanted to be with these guys just to hear from Annie but was hesitant for fear his disguise would show. His desire for news overcame his reasoning, and he followed Nathan into the cafeteria. Tony had not arrived. They picked up their trays and began to make their order as Tony entered the door.

"We will secure a table, Tony," Nathan said smiling at Tony's apparently frustrated face.

"This has been a morning to remember!" Tony exclaimed and then began to relax as he ordered lunch.

Steven and Nathan had settled into their chairs when Tony came up with his tray.

"You guys are hungry by the looks of your trays," he commented. They all laughed in a relaxed manner.

After Tony blessed the food, the three began to eat. Conversation was easy among them. They first discussed their respective mornings, and then talk turned to the upcoming event. The party was foremost in Nathan's and Tony's minds. Steven was struggling with his desire to go.

"Christina says Annie has no idea of her surprise. She and Katie had lunch with her one day this week and had a blast," Nathan offered.

"Did Christina get around to the subject of the reason for Annie's apparent preoccupation?" Tony began to inquire. "I haven't called her since our night out last week. I want her friendship if that is all we can have." Tony was honest.

"Well I'm glad you feel that way, Tony. Christina did say Annie shared something that startled both she and Katie out of their boots," Nathan said.

"What was that? Are you allowed to pass it on without betraying a confidence?" Tony asked, hoping to hear something that would make sense of the whole situation.

Steven held his breath. . . . . . *What did the girls find out about Annie? What could she be preoccupied with? Was there someone new in her life? Was that why Tony was losing out with her?*

After swallowing a big bite, Nathan told them, "Christina did not seem to think she should not tell me, but I'm sure they don't want it published," Nathan said and laughed.

He went on, "Annie told them she had met someone, and this was Christina's words, 'that made her know she could not get serious about anyone else'."

Steven shivered and froze. The sandwich seemed like cardboard, and he was a little nauseated. He wondered when she met this person. Nathan was still talking -- he must listen.

"It seems she's not seeing the guy, and when I asked Christina why, she said because the guy was not a Christian, or rather he indicated he was not personally involved with Christ. He was brought up in the church but did not share the same faith that she did in the Lord," Nathan explained.

Steven was as one paralyzed. He thought his heart was going to stop beating. The air in the cafeteria was close, and he needed fresh air. He could not leave this conversation, but could he bear to stay and hear more?

"Did she say any more about him? Where they met? What he was like? What he did in the way of a profession?" Tony was really interested.

"Christina asked where they met, and Annie said . . . . . ." Just at that moment someone came up to the table.

It was Terri. "Well, hello, are you guys having a serious discussion?" Steven wanted to choke her. He had to hear the answer to this question.

"I'm afraid we are, Terri," Steven said with irritation in his voice.

She looked at him with a wicked smile and said, "Dr. Billups, you need a rest. I think you are working too hard."

With this she left the table and went through the swinging doors of the cafeteria.

"Thanks for that, Steven. That lady can be a nuisance," Tony said.

"To get back to the account," Nathan said, "this is the most remarkable thing about all this. It seems he was one of her guards at the Manor."

Nathan noticed that Steven was white as a sheet and was having trouble breathing.

"Are you all right, Steven? I believe the lady is right. You are working too hard. Too bad when an accountant has to diagnose for the doctor," Nathan said with joking in his voice.

"I'll be all right, guys. This morning has been demanding."

Not nearly as demanding as lunch, thought Steven. He felt he had to be alone to contemplate the news he had just heard. He wanted to think, but how could he? He ran his fingers through his dark hair and shook his head in disbelief. Nathan and Tony had turned their conversation to the party. He knew, now, he could never go with them, but how he wanted to. Just to see Annie, he thought.

He had missed her.

Steven stood up, picked up his tray and emptied it. He said his good-byes and walked out of the cafeteria.

Nathan watched him go, in earnest. "What do you suppose is wrong with Steven?" he asked Tony.

"I'm not sure; he could be pushing too hard. He is that kind of person, yet he seems so different these days. In school he was always the charmer of all charmers, never missing an opportunity to be involved in activities, parties and meeting new people. He was such a likable guy, full of fun and life. He is still likable, but has changed so much," Tony said with care for the guy. "Do you think we have left him out of the conversation, talking about Annie since he is not acquainted with her?"

"Well, he got rid of Terri for us as if he was interested to hear more," Nathan said.

It was past midnight before Steven had a breather. He went into the doctor's lounge on the pediatrics floor, hoping he could be alone. No one was in there, and he walked to the window that looked out on a garden. The moon was casting eerie shadows on the lawn. He was visualizing another lawn -- the lawn at the Manor. He was reliving a stroll to a big oak tree. The scent of blonde curls was evident, and the feel of a small soft hand in his big one could almost be felt now. The sweetness of the girl at his side was so real to him . . . . . . and the ecstasy of the kiss. *Oh, Annie, we are so far apart.*

All the things Nathan had shared at lunch flooded his mind, and his body became weak just thinking about that beautiful person, so kind, so tender and caring, and so in love. *Was she in love with Jason? Was it him? It could be Jason. No, Jason was a Christian. He had told him so. It couldn't be Louis or Ramsey. No, from the conversation, it was him . . . . Steven Billups.*

Warmth rushed through his body. Did he even dare to think it was true? He had not even called her because he knew she would not see him. She had told him she wanted someone in her life who shared the same measure of faith, or even more than she had. What should he do?

He had been thinking about all she had said to him about spiritual things, but he had just hardened his heart against them. He knew how she prayed for what she wanted. *Was she praying for him now?* Who could he turn to for help? There was Jason -- would he still be on duty?

Jason's assistant told Steven that he had left the hospital for the night and would not be on duty tomorrow. *Now, who could he go to? What had he read when he had seen the piece of paper Annie had given Jason?* He could not remember. *What about Tony?* Steven called down on the medical floor to learn that Tony was not due in until seven in the morning. Nathan would be gone as the office only staffed a skeleton crew for the night. He would have to wait. He heard his page to go to the room of a very ill child whom he had spent several hours with. He left the lounge to attend to this child.

Steven was hungry as he had not stopped for even coffee during the night. He took off his whites and splashed water on his face in an effort to give it some life, and then he made for the elevator. A cup of hot coffee would rejuvenate him, so he headed for the cafeteria. The elevator stopped on the surgery floor, and Tony got on, unaware of Steven. Tony turned to see another passenger in the elevator.

"My goodness, man! You look bushed," Tony said with concern in his voice.

"Are you on duty yet?" Steven asked.

"I was not due in until seven but was called in earlier because one of the guys came down with a virus," Tony said.

"That's okay, I'm leaving the hospital anyway." Steven seemed to be walking in a fog. Then he said, "I'll see you guys later." With this the elevator stopped and Steven stepped out.

The morning was cold and dreary. The snow was due to move in, and the city was blanketed with grey skies. Traffic moved slowly trying to avoid an accident. Even I-81 was moving slower than usual. It appeared the people were dreading to reach their destinations. It would have been a good day to stay inside, but life had to go on, and the essential thing that faced Steven was a thing he had looked forward to with mixed emotions.

He wanted to get it over with and dreaded the thought of it. He had been on duty all night but felt energetic with the task before him. He had phoned ahead and made an appointment and was hoping now to make the office in the appointed time with traffic as it was. Despite the gloom of the weather, his spirits were soaring and had been since early morning. He had a mission and was anxious to accomplish it.

He turned off the interstate and took the street he was directed to take. Parking his car, he reached for his gloves and rushed into the massive office building. He was told to go to the third floor and there would be a receptionist to direct him to the right office.

CHAPTER THIRTY

The waiting room of the North Country Women's Clinic was filled with young women from their early teens to those who could be grandmothers.

The team of doctors here had a good practice, thought Annie. She wondered how many of these women were here for abortions, as that practice was not limited to abortion. How sad, she thought, that many of these people do not know the truth.

She picked up a magazine as she waited to be recognized by the receptionist. There had been a steady stream of patients since she had arrived. Looking up, she saw an opening to the desk and felt it was time to make her move.

Stepping to the receptionist's desk, she announced her name to the astonishment of the dark-haired, dark-eyed girl. The receptionist must have recognized my name by my father's reputation, thought Annie. The girl at the desk appeared very nervous.

Annie, not wishing to cause any problem to the girl, calmly said, "I am here to see a friend of mine." This seemed to upset the girl even more. Annie continued, "Darlene Gray."

Before she could say any more the girl's expression changed to one of shock.

"You? . . . Darlene's friend?" She looked as if she could not believe her ears.

"Yes, would it be possible for me to see her? I will only be a minute," Annie said with a smile spreading from her blue eyes across her face.

"Sure, the second door to the left. She is filing some charts," the dark girl said never taking her eyes off Annie.

Annie tapped lightly on the door of the designated room. A voice inside said, "Come in."

Without looking up Darlene then said, "Is there something I could do for you?"

"You can speak to your friend," Annie said with kindness in her voice.

Darlene's mouth fell open, and she could not believe what she was actually seeing. The girl had been serious about having her for a friend. She had wondered if they would ever meet again. Darlene stopped filing and motioned for Annie to sit down in the chair directly in front of the large desk.

"I'm sorry, I am speechless," Darlene said with all honesty.

"Because I came by to see you or because I am here?" Annie laughed.

"Both, I guess."

Darlene looked prettier today than ever. Her auburn hair was shining and had been trimmed in a lovely style to compliment her oval face. The green eyes that looked directly into Annie's blue ones were more confident. Something was taking place in this girl's life, thought Annie.

"I came by to ask you to lunch tomorrow," Annie said.

"You mean it?" Darlene was shocked.

"Why would I not mean it, Darlene? I told you at the Manor that I wanted you for a friend," Annie persisted. "You do have a lunch hour, don't you?"

"Yes, though sometimes I snack here and don't leave the office," Darlene said.

"Well tomorrow I will pick you up at, say . . . twelve. Is that okay?" Annie was smiling at the pleased look on Darlene's face.

"That's just great."

Darlene was still amazed.

"I better let you get back to work now. See you then."

With this Annie pushed the strap of her purse over her shoulder and opened the door and was gone. As she went through the waiting room, she noticed the eyes of the dark-haired girl were still staring at her.

The next day Annie was excited to lunch with Darlene. She was encouraged with the change she was seeing take place in the girl. Her appearance had drastically changed. Instead of the tight clothes she had worn at the Manor, Darlene had on a pretty peach cotton sweater and a dark forest green slim skirt that did not cling to her body. Annie did not know to what extent her heart had changed, but she knew there was something going on inside this friend.

Annie arrived about two minutes before twelve, and as she drove up to the curb, Darlene rushed out the door of the clinic and into the Toyota. They drove to a little restaurant not more than two blocks away so they would have plenty of time to talk. The food had been good when Annie had come to this restaurant with her mother.

They found a little table with a red-checked cloth on it and a basket full of all sorts of crackers. They had fun sampling the crackers and listening to the soft music until the waiter came to take their order.

Annie, looking over the menu, said, "I believe I will have shrimp scampi and garden salad with iced tea, please."

The waiter looked at Darlene. Darlene ordered a grilled chicken breast with rice pilaf and pineapples and iced lemonade. When the waiter left, the girls got down to their conversation.

"Tell me what has been happening with you," Annie said. "You look so pretty."

"I never dreamed I would see you again. I thought when you were released to go home you would try to forget all of us at the Manor." Darlene was still toying with the absurd idea of Annie wanting her to be her friend.

"It has taken me a little time to get my mind back into school and into the swing of life, but I intended to see you sooner or later. I told you I wanted to be your friend at the Manor," Annie said convincingly.

"I see that now," Darlene said with a smile, the first real smile Annie ever remembered seeing on her face.

"What about you and Louis?" Annie asked, noticing that Darlene lowered her eyes at the question.

"Louis is leaving Watertown. He said I was different. He thinks it has something to do with you," Darlene said, finally looking at Annie.

"Does this bother you a lot, Darlene?" Annie asked ignoring Louis's accusation.

"That he is leaving?" Darlene asked Annie.

"Yes," Annie said hoping to hear that it did not.

"Well, at first it did, and then I found out that Louis's friendship did not mean as much to me as it once had. I guess because I found that I had other people who wanted to be my friend, and, you know, the verses you shared with me. I have tried to pray and ask Jesus to be my friend."

Darlene is so close to committing her life to Christ, thought Annie.

"Do you believe He is your friend?" Annie asked.

"I am finding it hard to have a positive attitude about Him wanting to be, but I bought a Bible and in it I read that He loved a woman named Mary Magdalene or something like that. And she sounded even worse than me," Darlene said with laughter in her eyes.

"That's right, and you remember I told you all of us had sinned," Annie said.

"I read every day and pray like I heard that you do. You shook everybody up at the Manor with your Bible reading and prayer."

Darlene laughed, and Annie thought what a lovely person she was.

"When is Louis leaving?" Annie asked, thinking he had lost his hold over Darlene.

"I'm not sure. I don't see him except when he comes by the clinic. He doesn't work for Dr. Ramsey anymore. There are a lot of changes taking place there."

Annie did not ask about that, feeling her father would share with her anything significant.

"There will be someone else come into your life, Darlene," Annie said convincingly.

"That is what Dr. Ramsey told me," Darlene said. Then she told Annie that Dr. Ramsey had offered to send her to college and to let her help in the clinic also so that she would have spending money for herself. This made both the girls happy.

Before their lunch was over, a concrete friendship was established, and Annie had invited Darlene to church, offering to come by and pick her up the next Sunday. Darlene was eager to go. Annie had told her about the group of people around their age that was always getting together and wanted her to be a part of that group. She promised to call at the office when they planned their next gathering.

Annie drove Darlene back to the clinic, and they laughed all the way about one thing or another. Just before they got to the clinic, Darlene reached into her purse and unwrapping a little package, she lifted a tiny gold cross suspended on a tiny gold chain and held it out to Annie.

"I have held this so many times in the past few weeks and thought about what you said. 'Open when you are lonely and need a friend.'

When I opened the package and saw this little gold cross, I was reminded of the things you shared with me about Jesus. I want you to have this back as I know someone special gave it to you," Darlene said with feeling.

"That is your gift from me, Darlene. That was all I could give you as a token of our friendship and to remind you that not only I loved you but the One who once hung on a cross, but does no longer, loves you. It was given to me by my parents when I was a little girl, but when I was thinking about you I felt God was prompting me to give it to you." Annie finished as she parked.

She turned her head to look at Darlene, and tears were streaming down her cheeks. She wrapped the tiny cross in the same piece of paper that Annie had first given her and tucked it safely in her purse.

"I will see you Sunday, Darlene," Annie said as Darlene left the car and made for the door of the clinic. She turned and waved to her new friend before Annie started the engine of the car.

CHAPTER THIRTY-ONE

Saturday morning proved to be a glorious morning. The snow clouds had moved out on Friday leaving the city with a promise of a pretty weekend. Annie spent some time this morning catching up on some letters she had needed to write and getting her room in order after the busy week. She had especially enjoyed her devotion this morning as she read from Psalm 37.

She always took one verse as God's promise, and today her promise was verse four, "Delight thyself also in the Lord; and He shall give thee the desires of thine heart." She felt she had no right to apply that promise to what she was feeling for Steven. But she knew she could hold on to it concerning Steven giving his heart to Christ.

How she had prayed for him the past few weeks! It had seemed like forever since she last saw him. Often her thoughts reviewed the events of her time spent at the Manor. She picked up the phone and dialed the number of the Manor. She had not spoken to Sally since she had left. Life had been so full since her return home.

The morning passed quickly at the Marrow household as most Saturday mornings did. When the family sat down for lunch, Annie shared some of her conversation with Sally with her parents.

"I am looking forward to meeting her. Do you think we could arrange that soon, Annie?" Julia inquired.

"Sure, Mother, I did promise Sally I would come out one day for a visit. I would love for you and Dad to see the Manor. It is very beautiful. When I had settled down a little, I thought about how you would have liked it. That is, under any other circumstances."

Annie seemed distant at times just thinking about her stay there.

The afternoon was filled with various guests dropping by, and around two c'clock the telephone rang. Andrew answered it and came into the living room to announce that Jody was on the phone and wanted to speak with Annie. Annie was elated at the thought of speaking with him. It was the first time Annie had talked with Jody since her return.

When she came back into the living room her face was glowing as she recounted her conversation with her "brother." They had a good time discussing the various episodes of Annie's childhood and memories of Jody.

"He has really nailed some things down. That is thrilling about his commitment to Christ," Annie said almost absently. She was thinking of someone else who needed to make the same commitment.

"What are you wearing to dinner tonight?" Julia was asking, bringing Annie back to the present.

"Well, I have the new dress we had bought for my dinner before. I guess that's what I will wear," Annie said. She had not thought about it until then.

"I was thinking either the cream dress with the pale pink roses or the blue chiffon would be nice," Julia suggested.

Annie looked at her mother with a rather blank stare. Her thoughts were on the night she wore the blue chiffon. She could visualize Steven's face when he first saw her in that dress and during dinner as she looked across the table and caught his eyes with her own.

"I haven't thought about either of those. I suppose the other dress would be nice to save for Christmas," Annie said.

Annie took a lot of time getting her bath for the dinner at Riverside. She needed to relax in the apricot bubblebath that had been sent over from the Manor. As she was in the tub she thought about another evening and the care she had taken getting dressed for dinner. Slipping into her robe to apply her makeup, she looked at the solemn face in the mirror. She decided she needed to spend some careful consideration to her makeup tonight.

She wanted to look her best, as her parents had gone to a lot of trouble to reschedule her dinner at Riverside. She had tried to persuade Christina and Nathan to join them, but they said they had plans.

After applying her base coat she tried to get her blush just right. Her paleness needed to be camouflaged. The little brush of eye shadow brought out her big bright blue eyes. Annie ran a soft pink lipgloss over her lips for the total effect. Her blonde curls gleamed.

As Annie came down the stairs, her parents were in the foyer on the telephone. They thought she was the most beautiful person they had ever seen. She had chosen the blue chiffon, and as the soft full skirt fell around her legs, she looked as if she was floating.

"It's a pity to waste all that beauty on your old dad," Andrew teased with admiration showing in his eyes.

"We had better get going," Julia said. "Weren't our reservations at seven, Andrew? You can never tell how the traffic is going to be on Saturday night."

"You're right. Are my two lovely ladies ready?" he asked helping first Julia into her coat and then Annie into a pretty white coat she had received on her last birthday.

The drive to Riverside was pleasant. There were a lot of drivers on the road, but Andrew was a competent driver and maneuvered his car well. They talked constantly, enjoying the time spent together. The night was proving to be a good one.

The moon had not made its appearance on the horizon, but the night should be one to remember.

The conversation turned to a breakfast meeting Andrew had had with Dr. Ramsey just this morning. This had become a habit, and they had found a lot to discuss. Even though they disagreed on a lot of things, Andrew did not give up. He told Annie that Ramsey had said he was giving some thought to what she had said about abortions at one of the dinners.

"I think God is working in his life. He is not there yet, but with prayer and patience, I believe he is giving it some thought," Andrew said optimistically.

"That would be wonderful," Annie said, but her thoughts immediately turned to someone else. Andrew pulled into the parking space that had just been vacated by another car close to the entrance and helped the two ladies out. Walking into the restaurant, he spoke to the hostess who met him with a big smile. She was a tall auburn-haired girl dressed in a simple black dress. Her hair was piled on top of her head, and at her ears were dangling diamond earrings.

"Hello, Mr. Marrow," she said. "Looks like you are right on time." She picked up a clipboard and motioned for them to follow her.

"I decided to put you in the private dining room. You had told me this was a special evening in honor of your daughter," she said with a big smile.

The three followed her, Andrew dropped behind, and Julia walked beside him. Annie was the first to step into the room as the auburn-haired girl opened the door wide.

"SURPRISE!" echoed in Annie's ears. A chorus of hellos and laughter resounded.

A big smile spread across Annie's face as she could see dimly in the candlelight many of her closest friends. Christina and Nathan, Tony and Katie, and there was Jason. There were others. Kimberly Johnson and Abigail Burns and their dates were the first to reach her.

"Well, we finally get to pull this off," they said to Annie.

"Yes, we have waited a long time." Abigail said and smiled and kissed Annie on the cheek.

Tears were being blinked back from Annie's eyes as she looked back at her parents. All this time she had thought she was going to spend the evening with them, and they had known all along that her closest friends were in on the surprise.

Nathan and Christina moved forward, and behind them were Tony and Katie and someone else . . . she could not make out who. There was just a shadow of a person behind Nathan. Nathan was so tall. Jason was also in the group.

Christina hugged Annie and exclaimed how beautiful she looked. Annie twirled around in a playful way giving them the full effect of her dress. Katie and Christina both acted as if they hated to move away from her. These three had shared a lot of birthday celebrations.

Nathan and Tony, moving in closer, stood to the left of Annie and said, "We have someone we want you to meet, Annie."

In Annie's excitement she hardly saw the person they were referring to as she was listening to Christina's and Katie's conversation.

"Finally, I am introduced to you properly," the tall handsome young man said.

Annie's pulse pounded in her ears, and her heart acted as if it would beat out of her chest. She looked into the bluest eyes she had ever seen, fringed with dark curly lashes, and she could not turn her eyes away. He was smiling at her and gave the appearance to her and all present that they had never met before. *What was he doing here? How did he get invited? Of course, at the Good Samaritan.* But . . . then sketches of conversation came back to her. He had asked her about Nathan and Tony the day of the picnic. She was brought back to the present and found his hand was still holding hers. He did not appear in a hurry to let it go. She had reached out to shake his hand in the introduction, and he still held it. Their eyes were still locked, and time stood still. It felt as if they were the only people in the room.

Annie could hear him as he was saying, "It seems you make quite an impression, Miss Marrow."

Why was he acting like this, Annie wondered. *Why did he not just say that they had met before? What difference did it make? He was here.*

"He's a real charmer, Annie, watch him," Nathan was saying slapping Steven's shoulder.

"Thanks for the warning, Nathan. I can see he could be," Annie said and tried to regain her composure.

Steven finally let go of Annie's hand, stepping to the side in order that her other guests could speak to her but not getting very far away.

Jason stepped up and gave Annie a knowing smile. He kissed her in a sisterly way on the forehead and whispered, "Hello, sister."

After all the greetings were given, the group began to be seated. Annie was sitting at the table with her parents. There were large round tables seating eight at each table. At their table were Nathan and Christina, Katie and Tony, and, of all people, Steven.

It happened that her parents were on each side of Annie, and directly in front on the other side of the table was Steven. Annie felt she could not eat a bite that would stay down. Each time she raised her eyes they were looking directly into his. She felt she was drowning in their dark blue pools.

Steven spoke to her, "Annie, how is school?"

"Fine, I am finally caught up," she answered.

Much conversation was made by the young people as well as Annie's parents. Steven shared about his busy life at the hospital. Nathan and Tony told a funny incident they had been involved with, and the evening progressed in spite of Annie's emotional roller coaster feeling.

The food was delicious, prime rib with all the trimmings. They were ready for dessert before she knew it, and being wheeled into the dining room was a beautiful decorated cake in her honor. It was iced in chocolate embossed in pale pink with shades of pink roses clustered around it. The waiter began to cut it, and the entire group joined in with their rendition of "Happy Birthday."

Coffee was served, and after the cake had been eaten, Andrew rose from his chair and thanked the group for coming to help them celebrate with Annie. They all clapped and began to mingle while slipping into their coats.

Steven rushed to Annie's chair with her coat, and she slipped her arms into the sleeves. His hand brushed hers as he let go, and excitement spread through her body. She heard him catch a deep breath.

Close to her ear he whispered, "You look even more beautiful than the last time you wore this blue creation."

"Perhaps that is because I am free," she said.

Andrew came up to Steven and invited him to ride with them to their home as a few of the couples were going there to enjoy fellowship further.

Annie was shocked at her father. This was not out of character, but could he not see the effect this man had on his daughter? Annie smiled at Steven as he turned to her after the invitation.

The ride back to the Marrow's home was a pleasant one. Andrew asked Steven a lot of questions about his position at the hospital. How long would it be before he would venture out into private practice? He even asked about his parents and family.

Annie heard some of the conversation, but she was so preoccupied with the awareness of Steven's presence that she could not concentrate on facts. There was more than a physical attraction; Annie came to realize they were drawn together in other ways.

Julia told Steven how happy they were to meet him and asked how he had come to get acquainted with Nathan and Tony. Annie sensed Julia knew more about Steven than she, herself, had realized.

Steven slipped his hand over and picked up Annie's small one in his, giving it an affectionate squeeze. It seemed so natural at the Manor, but here she felt so aware of him -- and the effect he had on her emotions. They were turning into the drive and into the garage.

Andrew sprang from the car to open the door to admit the happy party goers. It had been such a success, and he was certain the rest of the evening was going to be even better. These kids had always loved the fellowship in the Marrow home, and now there were two new ones to join the group. I am impressed with Steven, Andrew thought.

Steven helped Annie from the car and into the foyer. He took her coat from her, as Julia rushed to gather the coats to be hung in the closet. The guests went naturally into the living room and began to take their places. They all felt as much at home here as they did in their own homes. They were chatting happily.

Steven did not leave Annie for one minute. All the time Annie was so aware of him that she had fallen silent. She had not been this way before, she thought. *She must make an effort to come out of this spell.*

Annie could see Christina and Katie looking at her strangely. They were probably wondering what was happening to her. *Did they know what effect this handsome man was having on her emotions?*

Annie and Steven were sitting together on the loveseat along with Jason. Annie noticed that Jason had not given away the secret that she knew Steven. What was going on? She asked herself. Steven's shoulder was touching hers, and she sighed softly.

He turned his smile on her as he caught hold of her hand sending a thrill through her body, and said for only her to hear, "You don't have to worry about the guy holding your hand not being a Christian anymore."

His eyes were looking deeply into hers for her reaction to his words. A look of utter surprise caused her eyes to light up, and tiny crinkles began to form around them. A smile touched her lips and spread over her face.

"What are you saying?" she whispered breathlessly.

"Just that you told me you would not date anyone who was not a Christian and that the man you wanted to share your life with must share your faith in God," Steven said, not daring to take his eyes away.

"Now I qualify." He laughed softly.

Steven could see the joy his news brought to her.

"Oh, Steven, that's great," was all Annie could say. Tears were filling her eyes.

The other guests noticed the two and were puzzled at the familiarity between them, all except Jason. He was bubbling with joy. He knew how Annie felt about Steven from the day she had met him.

"Hey, you two, let us in on the secret," Nathan said jokingly. Wow, he thought, this Steven moves fast!

"Should we, Miss Marrow?" Steven asked teasingly to Annie, squeezing her hand.

Annie could only nod, breathless . . . still looking at Steven.

"Okay, we will," Steven said. He seemed to take possession of the situation at this time. Annie watched him, wondering just what he was going to say or do.

All eyes and ears were turned to Steven, even those of Annie's parents. They exchanged glances as Steven began to speak. Still holding onto Annie's hand, Steven inched forward on the loveseat.

"There is something I must tell you, and I hope you will still let me be your friend," Steven began. "I had met Annie before tonight."

The group was startled. Nathan and Tony looked at each other in bewilderment. They were stunned by this announcement.

Christina and Katie exchanged knowing glances -- slapping their hands over their mouths.

Steven looked at Tony and Nathan. "I will get to you two later."

Then he went on. "Dr. Ramsey asked me to do a little job for him. I thought it would prove to help me and give me a little prestige with the man. I was of the opinion that I needed him to further my career in pediatrics."

He paused to look at Annie. She smiled at him, their eyes locking for an instant, both remembering their conversation.

"So I accepted his offer. I had no idea of the extent of the plans.

When I went to the Manor to serve as a companion to a young woman, that was his way of putting it, I met Annie Marrow."

He squeezed her hand and looked her in the eye. Annie returned his look with a smile curling her lips.

She was remembering how they first met . . .

"You want to tell them how we met?" Steven asked teasingly.

"Not now," she said, a blush spreading over her pretty face.

"After spending some time with her and realizing what an unusual person she was, I was in awe. She had boldness to tell me just what I was, and I was angry with her, but the sweet spirit that emanated from her, that now I know to be the spirit of Christ, really got my attention. I thought when she was released to go home I could shake her memory and the miserableness of my condition, but I was not able to do so and just hardened my heart against everything she said. Annie's faith intrigued me, but I was afraid of it for myself. When she was released, I knew there was no chance of seeing her as she had told me the kind of man she wanted to share her life with, and I knew I could never be that man."

Steven stopped and looked at Nathan and Tony, who were mesmerized by what they were hearing.

"I must ask Nathan and Tony to forgive me as I used their friendship to my advantage. I overheard them in the cafeteria one day, and they mentioned Annie's name. I found out that the girl they mentioned was the same person who had upset my life with her love for God. So when Annie came home, the only way I could know what was happening in her life was to be with them."

Steven bowed his head before looking at Nathan and Tony again.

"Will you guys forgive me for this?" he asked sincerely.

Tony and Nathan were so stunned they could hardly believe what they were hearing.

Tony finally gained his composure and answered, "Sure, Steven." He reached over and patted Steven's shoulder.

Nathan, brought back from his numbness by Christina's elbow in his ribs, said, "Man, no wonder you looked like a ghost when we talked about her. We were worried about you working too long and hard." Nathan then chuckled.

"But that's not all," Steven went on. "Annie had told me that I was good at wearing a mask."

When he paused to glance at Annie, Nathan took it up with "I'll say you are!"

Nathan's joking manner brought a laugh from the group and relaxed the tensions that were in the room.

"I was brought up in a Christian home, but as Annie put it so plainly to me, I only knew about God, He was not personal to me. I saw how personal He was in her life. She actually depended on Him. When she read His Word she believed it. That upset me! It took that to make me think. Last Thursday morning I became so distraught that I tried to reach Jason because he had just committed his life to Christ, and I thought he could help me. He was not in the hospital. Then I thought about Tony. I knew he had hours similar to those of mine but was told he would not be in until seven in the morning. I survived the rest of the morning until I left the hospital."

Tony gave Steven a knowing look as he remembered their conversation in the elevator.

"I knew I had to go to Mr. Marrow and ask for his forgiveness -- I knew where Mr. Marrow worked from Annie, so I made an appointment. While I was there he saw my real need and led me to Christ. He reiterated what Annie had said, that I had been wearing a mask."

"I no longer wear a mask, Annie." Their eyes met in love.

Then as if they were the only people in the room Steven said, "Tonight when Nathan and Tony introduced us, it was the first time you had met me as I am -- a new person." He squeezed her hand and smiled into her eyes.

"Now tell us how you met, Annie," Katie said as though she had not heard a word that was spoken.

"Maybe I will sometime," Annie said.

"All I will say," Steven said, "is that no one told me I would enter a combat zone when I went to guard her."

The group really thought that was funny.

Julia, sensing that Annie and Steven needed to be alone, suggested they go into the kitchen and make hot chocolate for the guests. A knowing smile crossed their faces as the couple jumped from the loveseat and left the others with their conversation and comments on the news they had just heard.

In the kitchen, Steven slipped his arms around Annie and pulled her close. She knew this was where she wanted to stay for always.

He kissed her soundly and sweetly and then he said, "You have a very discerning mother."

They both laughed.

"I believe I am the happiest person alive," Annie whispered. "I'm glad that mask is gone. I have prayed for you -- I like the real Steven Billups best of all."

"Have you thought about me too?" Steven asked with a gleam of mischief in his eyes. He was running water in the tea kettle to put on the stove as Annie was spooning chocolate into the cups.

"Yes, I did not want to, but I could not help but think about you," Annie said, looking at his handsome face.

"Annie, I love you so much. I thought you were the most beautiful girl I had ever seen, lying there asleep. I realize I have loved you since we first met. You were so sincere and sweet and yet strong and bold in your circumstances. I had never met anyone like you. I could not explain my feelings. I wanted to be with you, and I wanted to be away from you because you could see right through me." Steven put his arm around her and kissed her on the forehead.

"I did not want to admit that I loved you. I knew I would not be able to go out with you as you were, and yet I could not forget you and the loving way you planned special things for me," Annie said sweetly.

"Do you know what I thought when I opened my eyes that morning and saw you?"

"What?" asked Steven.

"That you were the handsomest guy I had ever seen."

"Your dad saw my need and got right to the point with me. He seems to like me. He has offered to talk to the board at the placement home that is being built about my being the doctor for the babies that are to be adopted," Steven said.

He pulled Annie into his arms again and kissed her. He hated to release her.

They loaded the trays with cups of piping hot chocolate and made their way back to the living room.

As they entered the room, Nathan teasingly said, "You guys took an awfully long time to make instant hot chocolate. Annie, you better watch this guy - he has a reputation around the hospital. They call him a charmer of all charmers."

The group laughed.

"Listen, this little girl can outdo me any day with that title. She had everybody at the Manor charmed," Steven said lovingly.

He put the tray on the coffee table and then put his arm around Annie as he whispered, "A charming hostage."

Jason spoke up with, "She even charmed Dr. Ramsey. I bet Jake Ramsey will remember the dinner he invited her to. She kept the ball in her court all night. I have never seen him so speechless. It was a reversed hostage situation."

They all laughed at this.

"In fact, Dr. Ramsey's hostage took us all hostage with her charm," Steven teased.

Annie could only thank God for what He had done. She was

thinking about the Psalm she had read this morning -- "Delight thyself in the Lord and He shall give thee the desires of your heart."

Printed in the United States
43417LVS00004B/136-144